She'd been so naive,
Flame thought

The only freedom she'd ever really wanted had been the freedom to love Marlow forever. Now, unable to bear the look on his face, she turned to the door.

"Wait!" Marlow didn't raise his voice but the note of command made her pause. "Let's get one thing clear, Flame. I'm not letting you go without a fight. As far as I'm concerned you're still my wife."

"Merely in order to please your mother-in-law?" she said scathingly.

"Obviously not. Though I'd like to please her—she's a lovely woman. But there are other considerations. I want what's mine." His voice shook and he came around the desk toward her, his face sharply etched with the intensity of his anger.

"You're on my territory now, Flame. And I'm going to make sure you remember it!"

SALLY HEYWOOD is a British author, born in Yorkshire. After leaving university, she had several jobs, including running an art gallery, a guest house and a boutique. She has written several plays for theater and television, in addition to her romance novels for Harlequin. Her special interests are sailing, reading, fashion, interior decorating and helping in a children's nursery.

Books by Sally Heywood

Don't miss any of our special offers. Write to us at the following address for information on our newest releases.

Harlequin Reader Service
P.O. Box 1397, Buffalo, NY 14240
Canadian address: P.O. Box 603,
Fort Erie, Ont. L2A 5X3

SALLY HEYWOOD

simply forever

Harlequin Books

TORONTO • NEW YORK • LONDON
AMSTERDAM • PARIS • SYDNEY • HAMBURG
STOCKHOLM • ATHENS • TOKYO • MILAN

Harlequin Presents first edition December 1991
ISBN 0-373-11417-6

Original hardcover edition published in 1990
by Mills & Boon Limited

SIMPLY FOREVER

CHAPTER ONE

FLAME swung round when she heard the door of her office open. It was Johnny, boss of the exhibition consultants she was working for. He took one look at her face and was across the room at once, concern evident in the searching look he gave her.

'Sweetie, what is it?' he exclaimed.

She side-stepped the hand he put out, crumpling the airmail letter by her side as she did so, and giving a little shake of her head at the same time. 'Just a letter from my sister,' she muttered.

'Bad news?'

She nodded reluctantly. 'I guess so.' And when Johnny went on looking down at her she was forced to add, 'It's Mother. She's been ill for several weeks, but it looks as if she's taken a turn for the worse.' She raised green eyes, her face pale in its frame of red-gold hair. 'I'm not sure how serious it is. Samantha's the last person to panic, but reading between the lines she seems to want me to go home.'

'Home?'

'Back to Spain, I mean.'

Johnny pulled a face. 'I've never heard you call it that before.'

Flame turned away, her hands clenching involuntarily. 'I shan't go unless I really have to.' She gazed unseeingly out of the office window at the busy London

5

street below. Then she spun round to face him. 'Oh, Johnny, I know Samantha wouldn't suggest I went back unless she was really worried. But what shall I do? The last thing I want is to go back *there*, of all places!'

'If it's as serious as you imagine, surely she would have taken the trouble to ring you?' he suggested.

'Maybe she wanted to warn me gently?' Flame lifted her shoulders in a helpless shrug.

'You know your sister better than I do.' He took her by the arm before she could resist. 'Look, sweetie, stop worrying. There's the phone in front of you. Ring her now, set your mind at rest. It's probably nothing at all.'

She felt his fingers slide down her arm as she moved away. 'You're sweet, Johnny,' she said to mitigate her obvious reluctance to feel his touch. 'But I thought maybe I'd ring this evening when I get home——'

'Nonsense,' he corrected. 'I'm not sweet, you're the one who's sweet. I'm merely selfish. You'll be no use to me today if your mind's on other things. Now here's the code book.' He skidded it across the desk. 'Stop brooding and find out the facts.' He gave her a grey-eyed glance. 'I hope it's nothing serious, not only for the obvious reasons, but because——' he pulled a face '—put simply, I don't want to let you go.'

Despite his obvious attempt to make light of it there was a hint of some deeper emotion behind his words, and Flame knew instinctively that he was making more than just a reference to the workload they had on at present. She bit her lip, and he saved her from having to say anything by going purposefully through into his office adjoining her own.

There was a strange tension in her as she dialled the familiar number of the Villa Santa Margarita. She had always arranged with Samantha or her mother beforehand whenever she was going to give them a call, just to be on the safe side. Now she was nervous as she wondered who would pick up the phone at the other end. She steeled herself for that certain voice, but to her relief it was Samantha herself who answered.

'Darling,' began her sister at once, 'I'm so glad you rang! I was going to give you a bell myself tonight in case my letter hadn't got through.'

'It arrived this morning,' Flame told her. 'How is she?' she asked without preamble.

'Oh, Flame——' Samantha broke off, then her voice came again, calm with an effort. 'Listen, I won't beat about the bush. She wants to see you. She's fretting about not having seen you for so long and of course she's being terribly brave about it all and telling us not to worry. I really think you should drop everything and get over as soon as you can.' She added, 'You know I wouldn't be asking you to come haring back here if we weren't so desperately worried. Please say you'll try to make it——!'

'I'll come as soon as I can,' Flame broke in, her hands like ice.

'Sooner would be best——' Samantha's voice lifted half humorously, then choked to a stop. She seemed to make an effort to pull herself together and told Flame about the clinical tests they were waiting for. 'I don't want to scare you, Flame, that's why I wrote first.'

'I understand that, Sammy.' Unconsciously Flame used her elder sister's pet name, then, with a few words of reassurance that she knew could do little to help, she said she would start ringing round at once to try to book a flight. 'I'll call you tonight to let you know what time I'm arriving,' she told her sister.

One big question shrieked to be asked, but at the last minute her courage failed her. After enquiring about the children she replaced the receiver, then leaned against her desk for a long moment afterwards, appalled at her own cowardice.

Marlow. The name hammered in her head. They would *have* to meet. There was no escape now she was going back. No escape at all. But surely he wouldn't be so tactless as to come and meet her at the airport? Surely Samantha would arrange things differently, for by this time she must know how things still stood between them...

'All right?' Johnny was standing in the doorway of his office, a tentative smile on his face, breaking into her train of thought. When he saw her expression his smile faded at once, though. 'Not all right, I can see that.'

Flame shook her head, her eyes suddenly bright. 'I'm frightened, Johnny. Samantha sounded so unlike her usual bubbly self. She says Mother's had to have some tests at the clinic... It sounds serious, doesn't it?' It was difficult to imagine her pretty and vivacious mother as an invalid. Though she was in her early fifties now, Flame had always taken her mother's continued good health for granted. Her father had been the sickly one, moving to the warmer climate of southern Spain many years ago because of the recurring chest problem to which he had eventually succumbed some ten years ago.

'So you'll be going out there after all?' Johnny's eyes were already flicking to the data-day calendar on the wall beside her desk.

'I'm sorry. I know it's going to leave you in the lurch at the worst possible time——'

'That's not what worries me.' His grey eyes darkened for a moment, then he gave an off-beat smile. 'It can't be helped. Better get on to the agency and find me a temp, preferably one who can spell, remain civil in a crisis and make a decent cup of coffee. Do it first, then ring Transflight and ask for Tim.'

Flame jerked up her head.

'Not for me, idiot, for you,' he read her expression aright. 'If anybody can get you a flight at short notice, Tim can. Mention my name.'

Flame gazed at him without moving.

'Well, what are you waiting for?'

She shook herself. 'Your efficiency always leaves me speechless!' she tried to joke, but even as she did so she knew that Johnny had observed her hesitation and put two and two together.

He gave her a level glance. 'So you'll be meeting him, I take it?'

'I can hardly avoid it.' She gave a jerky laugh. 'It doesn't matter. It's not the end of the world...it just feels like it!' She was still trying to make light of the increasing tension she was feeling at what lay ahead, but Johnny wasn't fooled.

'Tell him you've met a wildly successful guy in London who's crazy about you——'

His voice unexpectedly thickened and he ran a hand rapidly through his spiky brown hair. 'Hell, I don't mean to come on all heavy, especially at a time like this. But I can't have you jetting back to him without a word about how I feel about you. You know I like to sort of hang loose...' He let his words tail off, gave her a lop-sided smile and went on hastily, 'You may have felt you're just one of the many at the moment, but it can't have escaped your notice that I think you're something pretty special. Flame?'

He moved closer, cupping her chin in his hand to tilt her face to his. This time she didn't flinch away, but her eyes warned him that the barricade was still up.

'You must have guessed by now how I feel,' he told her. 'And I think you must have guessed I'd have moved in on you long ago if I hadn't thought you'd slap me down pretty smartly if I did. I guess I'm hoping by the time your divorce comes through in six months' time you'll be as hooked on me as I already am on you.'

'Johnny,' Flame returned his smile as lightly as she could, breaking the intimacy of physical contact, 'I'm fond of you, and I really admire the way you've built this agency up. It's been great working for you. But you know, after what I went through with—with Marlow,' she faltered over the name even now, 'getting into any sort of relationship again is something I fight shy of.'

'I'm not pressuring, sweetie. But if things get tough out there, you know who you can run to.' Johnny ran a hand through his hair again, obviously embarrassed at losing his cool 'love 'em and leave 'em' pose for a moment, then he was back in familiar mode again. 'As I said, what are you standing about for? Go for it!' He swung back into his office as his own phone started to ring.

It was the beginning of another hectic day. But in between work Flame managed to fix a flight through Johnny's friend Tim, and at Johnny's insistence she rang Samantha again to let her know she would be arriving at five-fifteen in the morning. This time she forced herself to be sensible.

'I'll take a taxi from Malaga,' she said. 'I don't need anybody to pick me up from the airport.' She didn't have to elaborate on the 'anybody'.

'You'll have to face him some time, Flame,' warned Samantha. 'He's still part of the family.'

'Only for another six months.'

'Legally, yes, but in other ways for much longer than that . . .' Samantha sounded thoughtful. 'What I want to say, love, is he's still living at the villa, and for Mother's sake you're going to have to be civil to each other. You know how she feels about you both.'

'I'll be civil, don't worry. Nothing that rat can ever say or do will ever make me lose control again.' Flame spoke fiercely, convinced that at last she was over him. 'I'll be the perfect lady. Just don't let him be the one to meet me at the airport. I can face him, but not at five in the morning. Have a heart!'

'Emilio has already offered to pick you up, actually.'

'Still together?' Flame fell back on the standard joke.

Samantha chuckled despite the strain she was under. 'We've behaved stupidly in the past, but luckily we both admit it.'

'I always say crazy fools should stick together,' Flame quipped. As she replaced the receiver and began to throw a few clothes into a bag she felt a twinge of remorse at the obvious happiness in Samantha's voice. She and Marlow had blown their own chance of marital happiness eighteen months ago, and the chance of Marlow admitting the blame was zero.

Lucky Samantha! Things had turned out differently for her and her Spanish husband. They had had a yo-yo relationship at first, her sister's exuberant nature clashing openly and often with the volatile Latin temperament of her husband, and during the period before Flame's own marriage Samantha and Emilio were actually trying to live apart. But their problems had all blown over by the time Flame and Marlow had come to walk down the aisle. Reunited with her obviously adoring husband, Samantha had looked almost as radiant as the bride.

Deep down Flame knew the marriage was a good one, but one thing she couldn't forget, and that was how worried her mother had been throughout those years, as if she felt the break-up was a stigma on the whole family.

Flame had later come to see this attitude as one of the reasons her mother was so keen for *her* to marry, as if success in that direction for her younger daughter could conceal what she seemed to see as the failure of the elder one. But it wasn't entirely fair to say her mother had pushed her into marriage, for on top of that, of course, was the question of the land.

And on top of all that, if it wasn't enough, was the question of what now seemed to Flame her own senseless infatuation with Marlow Hudson himself. She had needed no encouragement to plunge headlong into marriage with him, she thought ruefully. She had been only too eager.

She went round the flat, checking that everything that should be switched off before she left was off. Bitter thoughts were running through her mind, and later, as the taxi sped towards the inevitable meeting with Marlow, she felt helpless to stop the flood of memories surging back. Until now she had ruthlessly repressed them, but with a meeting imminent she couldn't hold them back any longer. She remembered how she had left Spain, vowing never to return as long as Marlow Hudson remained uncrowned king of Santa Margarita. Now she was being forced to go back on that vow.

The whole issue of their marriage had been a recipe for disaster from the very beginning. Take one inexperienced nineteen-year-old, she thought wryly, and one power-hungry male, add in a rather large and undeveloped piece of real estate waiting for someone to exploit it and finally stir in one very impractical lady owner looking for a man to shoulder the burden.

She remembered the first time she had an inkling anything was afoot. 'All this will be yours one day, darlings,' her mother had told her and Samantha as they picnicked on the cliff top with the sweet-smelling pines sighing softly behind them and the broad, bright blue sweep of the sea caressing the tumbling cliffs. 'The trouble is I can't bear the thought of handing down nothing but a scrubby bit of undeveloped coastline to you both. Your dear father had such wonderful plans for it—gardens of pleasure and delight, not rocks and wilderness.'

'We like it,' Samantha had murmured, too intent on rubbing suntan oil into one of her toddlers' already golden limbs to pay much attention. Flame had nodded in agreement.

'But wouldn't it be wonderful if we could find someone to take charge of it for us and turn it into something really special?' Sybilla had argued, her eyes sparkling. 'What we want,' she went on to her unheeding daughters, 'is someone to take over all the boring facts and figures and transform the place into the paradise we used to dream about.'

The two girls, Flame herself little more than a year out of school, and Samantha in the first years of her then shaky marriage and more absorbed by that and her babies than anything else, agreed with what was being said. But neither of them could offer any practical way to turn the dream into reality.

It was then that Sybilla Montrose had drawn their attention to the man who had been systematically buying up the rest of the coastline around them. 'It would be very neat if he could finish off his game of Monopoly with the Cabo de Santa Margarita,' their mother had mused aloud, 'not that I could ever dream of selling, of course.'

'Mother, you wouldn't sell Santa Margarita?' exclaimed Flame.

'Never,' agreed Sybilla Montrose emphatically, 'but there may be other ways of getting what we want, my darling.'

There had been a gleam in her mother's eye that was nothing if not dynastic. It should have warned them that something was afoot. Too late Flame saw it all. By that time their mysterious saviour had a name and the legendary Marlow Hudson had become a frequent visitor at the villa.

Slowly but surely, she realised now, she had been set up: innocently by her mother, who only saw an excellent marriage to one of the most sought-after bachelors on the coast and the realisation of a dream as a result of her matchmaking—but, thought Flame, less innocently by Marlow Hudson himself. He, she was now convinced, had regarded the enviably sited Villa Santa Margarita with its extensive cliff-top gardens as a fitting dowry to accompany the child bride he was being offered. Once the wheels were set in motion things had moved with astonishing speed. They met and were married within six weeks.

Truly, thought Flame, she had been like a lamb led to the slaughter. It was madness to imagine a child of nineteen resisting the deliberate and practised charm of a man like Marlow. Ten years older than herself, he had led a cosmopolitan life that had given him a maturity beyond even that advantage. She had been dazzled, as he had meant her to be. And it sometimes seemed in those whirlwind days of courtship that he could actually read her mind, so closely did he seem to mould himself to her heroic image of him. She had been a puppet in his hands. Within days of their meeting he seemed to know everything about her, how best to exploit her innocent trust, how best to beguile her with the promise of unimagined heaven. She had grown desperate for him in ways her innocent heart had been unable to spell out. And she began to live every moment for the sight and sound of him.

She pulled herself up sharply, gathering her things angrily together in the back of the taxi. Even now, after all the pain that had followed shortly on the pleasure, she could become a helpless being of desire just thinking about him. Of course it was worse now than in those early days, for now she had the memory of the touch and taste and smell of him to taunt her imagination.

For a moment she was engulfed in a memory of his raw masculinity, something enhanced by the air of mystery surrounding him. It was a strange thing, but it wasn't until after she had left that she realised she knew so very little about him. She had been too much in love to care about his past. Now that she saw him clearly she realised he'd been an adventurer all along.

Cutting off the memory with a silent reproof, she alighted briskly from the taxi, paid the man off, then made her way into the station for the Gatwick connection.

As the distance between them narrowed, the ticking minutes passing her remorselessly from one stage of the journey to the next, she felt she was approaching a zone of infinite danger. But just to know how vulnerable she still was made her more sure than ever that she could never be so stupid as to yield to Marlow again.

The marriage is dead, she repeated, as the plane became airborne and the lights of England faded into the night. It died the day I discovered the truth.

In the eighteen months since she had fled he had made only one attempt to contact her, and that, she told herself, showed what he really felt for her. He had tracked her down through Samantha and made a brief phone call to ask her when she intended to return. She had repeated the gist of her farewell note, telling him marriage was a drag and she wanted to be free to be herself. It wasn't true, of course. Until that dreadful moment of truth marriage had been heaven. But it had been a fool's paradise, and pride had shown her the way out.

Since then the only news she had had from him had come via Samantha or, until recently, her mother. At best it had been sketchy and, she suspected, her mother's constant references to Marlow's desire to have her back owed more to Sybilla's own wishful thinking than to anything Marlow himself might have said.

Only two months ago she had told her mother, 'It's over, Mother, you must realise that by now. I have a new life in London, a good job, a nice flat. I don't need Marlow Hudson in my life ever again.' She had vowed never to return. But now she was being forced back.

The sign came on to fasten seatbelts as the plane hit a patch of turbulence. One or two worried glances flew between the passengers, but Flame closed her eyes with a sense of detachment. These days she was nothing if not a fatalist.

It was nearly an hour after that when she was roused by the announcement that they were approaching the Spanish coast. Soon a fairy-tale cluster of lights in the darkness below indicated the airport buildings, then the plane was racing between the avenue of landing lights and she knew with a sudden shock that she was once again on Marlow's territory.

Emilio was leaning on the barrier at the exit as she came bleary-eyed into the glare of the concourse. He seemed to pick out her slim, flame-coloured form at once, giving her a huge bear-hug in welcome as he took her bag. 'You've been missed, *cara*. This time you must stay for good.'

Flame kissed him on both cheeks. 'I've missed you all too. Whatever happened to your promised trip to England?' She knew how difficult it was for Emilio to leave his construction business. They chatted amiably as they walked back to the car. It was still dark, but by now there was a subtle glow of pearl on the eastern horizon, heralding a new day.

Throwing her bag into the back of the car, Emilio settled her into the passenger seat and began the drive through the sleeping suburbs of Malaga before taking the coast road to Santa Margarita.

'We'll stop at a bar when we're halfway,' he suggested, 'to give you chance to find your feet and time our arrival for breakfast!'

'A drink at six in the morning? Heavens, I've missed all that!' exclaimed Flame, remembering the summer holidays of old when they had all dined in the Spanish way at eleven, then danced till dawn, finishing with breakfast in cafés that never seemed to close.

Emilio must have been tipped off by Samantha, because he avoided mentioning Marlow altogether, and instead chatted amiably about his young family, proudly hinting at the likelihood of another baby.

By the time they drove in through the gates of Santa Margarita, the sky was a cloudless expanse of baby blue, as fragile as organza. The car climbed the steep driveway, with its border of royal palms, until at last the villa came in sight. Familiar though it was, Flame gave a small gasp. She would never get used to the natural beauty of its setting amid palms and cypresses and cascading vines, a setting enhanced by the perfection of the white-walled villa itself.

With its pleasing arrangement of arches and balconies and a roof terrace overlooking the bay, it was the result of her father's lovingly designed scheme to create a family home for his beloved wife and daughters. Everything about it was testimony to the lavish attention to their needs, from the spectacular gardens rising in a series of terraces on all sides, to the luxurious accommodation she knew lay within. Out of sight on the other side, within the privacy of the protective L of the building, was the main terrace and pool with breathtaking views of the Mediterranean as a backdrop.

Her gaze was drawn involuntarily to a smaller villa, half hidden among the trees. This had been her father's plan too—a gift for his eldest daughter, with further plans for an identical villa to be built lower down the headland when Flame came of age.

Samantha and Emilio had been the first occupants in the *casita*, as it was called, until Sybilla had persuaded them to move their growing brood into the far more spacious main house. It had stood empty for a while. Then, when Flame and Marlow married, they had moved into the *casita* themselves.

At Sybilla's instigation Marlow planned to complete Eric Montrose's designs for a second villa for Flame, and after its completion planned to move the nerve-centre of his property empire into the *casita*. Work had started on the new villa straight away. But then Flame had walked out.

As far as she knew all Marlow's plans had been put on ice, for she knew he still lived at the *casita*. She could glimpse it now through the pine trees lower down the hillside.

It was quiet when Emilio cut the engine. He lifted out her bag and walked with it towards the house. Flame got out and stretched for a moment. Slats of light broke through the branches of the trees, striping the path with light and shade. Her senses were assailed by the rich scent of hibiscus opening to the dawn.

She took a deep breath and turned with the intention of following Emilio inside, but a movement between the pines surrounding the *casita* caught her eye. She swivelled. There was nothing there, only sunlight re-claiming its domain with every passing second. She turned towards the house. Then something made her glance back again.

With a shudder she saw a familiar white-clad figure moving between the trees. The sight made her freeze. Marlow! It was useless to pretend she hadn't seen him.

She waited, carved in ice, as he came out on the path and walked deliberately towards her.

He must have heard the car drive up the hill, she told herself, her thoughts revolving with inexorable slowness. Perhaps he'd been out on the town and was just re-turning. Perhaps he always started work at this time. There was no other explanation for his appearance.

When he was still a few feet away he came to a stop as if some invisible barrier separated them. Her heart was bumping at the sight of him. Tall and broad-shouldered, with his gypsy-dark hair, he brought back an almost forgotten memory of physical power. An image flashed unbidden into her mind of strong arms coming round her to pick her up. It was on one of those days when she had felt herself truly loved, and she remembered how he had run with her in his arms into the waves on their beach in the cove below. She had revelled then in his physical power, mistakenly believing it would be hers forever.

Now he was standing within touching distance, but he didn't reach out. Instead he spoke her name, an upward, mocking inflexion in the sound, as if her arrival was unexpected. Then his eyes swept her face and they were as blue and empty and soulless as the sea.

'So you found something to bring you back?' he went on when she didn't return his greeting. He spoke in the familiar drawl that had once so thrilled her. This time, though, she was ready to resist it. Its seductive huskiness set up barriers this time around and she was prepared to fight it. Even so she heard herself stammer before managing to force out a proper reply.

'As you see,' she stiffened under his cool blue stare, 'I'm back. For Mother's sake.'

His eyes were something she'd thought she had forgotten—blue, turquoise, indigo, as pacific or storm-racked as the oceans. They stared into hers, provoking in their intensity. She couldn't drag her glance away, but nor could she bear the brunt of their scrutiny either without a thrill of unbidden desire prickling over her skin.

She stepped back, matching his assessment with one of her own. There was no doubt about it, he was wildly good-looking. She had quite forgotten just how black and thick was the hair she used to run her fingers through. His harshly honed features were tanned to a deep tropical gold, and his strong jaw and full, sensuous lips gave him a formidable air that could change at will into one of almost boyish charm. Oh, he had charm, she agreed coldly, but now she saw it as the deliberate ploy of a man who meant to get his own way at any price.

'Why didn't you warn me you were coming over?' he demanded.

'Did you need warning?' Flame raised a cool eyebrow.

'You know what I mean,' he said impatiently. 'Why no word?'

'It was all decided at the last minute,' she told him, as if it was no business of his. 'Surely Samantha told you?'

He nodded abruptly. 'I was away yesterday. She left a message on my answerphone last night.'

She was scarcely listening to what he said, her eyes raking over him with a sense of shock as all the old feelings sprang into life. His tan was enhanced by the stark white of his shirt. He had always worn white, she remembered. It had been his trademark. He told her it saved the bother of thinking what to put on because everything matched. Time, she remembered, had always been short. Marlow did everything at full pelt. At nineteen she had thought he looked glamorous in his white linen suit, like a film star.

Now she continued to give him an up-and-down look, one deliberately designed to show she was older now and unimpressed by such things. 'No doubt I'll see you around,' she clipped, backing away.

'Inevitably,' he remarked in a dry mocking tone as she turned to go.

Flame averted her head as she noticed his glance fall to her breasts, angry with herself for the blood that suddenly rushed to her cheeks as she read what that look meant. She forced herself to turn and walk steadily towards the steps, and when she paused at the top to look back she saw he was standing on the path, gazing after her—a motionless, enigmatic figure in white outlined against the growing crimson of the dawn sky. Despite how she felt about him there was a split second when something else overrode all other feelings, and she simply wanted to run to him, to plunge into the heart of the glowing scarlet sunrise, to be in his arms with the rough strength of him crushing her to him. But she knew it could never be, and the impulse was over almost at once. She slipped inside the house, closing the door firmly against such folly.

It was cool and dark inside, seeming more so because of the violent glow as the dawn sky filled with red. The old saying bit into her mind: red sky in the morning, shepherd's warning. Red was a danger warning even a child could understand. She was older now and not likely to forget it and make the same mistake twice.

CHAPTER TWO

FOR Flame the day had already begun, and it seemed pointless to go to bed now, so, after a peep into her mother's room which found her still sleeping, she breakfasted with Samantha and Emilio and their tiny trio in the large white and grey kitchen.

After Emilio had left for work the two women went out on to the terrace with the children. 'Mother sleeps late at the moment. She's very weak. Don't expect her to be her old self,' warned Samantha.

Then she introduced her sister to the live-in nanny, a capable-looking Swedish girl in her mid-twenties, and Flame greeted her warmly. Explained Samantha, 'Britt helps keep me sane in the face of the little monsters and their antics!'

'They are angels all three,' broke in Britt with a friendly smile.

'Did Emilio tell you about number four?' asked Samantha, turning to Flame.

She nodded, and something in her expression made Samantha take her by the arm and sit her down in one of the loungers by the poolside. 'Your face, love! It could be you, couldn't it, with a baby of your own? You should never have walked out on him.'

'I had no choice. Exit with dignity—that's what I did. And I'm glad. It was the right decision,' Flame said tightly.

'You seem so sure...'

'I am. One hundred per cent.' Yet she frowned.

'So what's worrying you?'

'Mother, of course,' she replied defensively. 'What else?'

Samantha regarded her younger sister closely. 'Can't you two kiss and make up after all this time? Surely it's not too late?'

'You must be mad, Sammy! After what *he* did?'

'What did he do, exactly? You weren't very forthcoming at the time.'

'You know damn well he couldn't be trusted!' It was true Flame had never gone into details. It had simply been too heart-wrenching at the time, and in the turmoil of pain that followed she assumed everyone knew the truth, for didn't they always say the wife was the last to know?

'I'm sure he was no worse than anyone else. After all, men will be men,' replied Samantha easily. 'What do you expect from somebody so outrageously attractive?'

'I expect the fidelity he expected of me,' replied Flame tartly. 'I don't accept double standards. Why should I?' Her stomach churned again at the memory of that terrible day when her heart had broken in two...

'Double standards. I suppose that's a dig at me?' Samantha raised luminous blue eyes to Flame's green ones.

'With you it was more than a double standard. From what I can make out you were both as bad as each other!' Flame tried to speak lightly and Samantha threw her head back in a throaty laugh.

'There was never anyone serious for either of us. It was just that we both liked to flirt and then we'd get horribly jealous and start shouting. I can tell you, we're both definitely reformed characters now!'

'So you don't accept a double standard either.'

Samantha smiled softly. 'I must admit I'd find it hard to go on if I thought Emilio preferred the company of other women.'

'Luckily you know he's crazy about you. It's obvious from everything he says and does.' The way Emilio had looked at his wife over the breakfast table showed plainly to Flame that his wild oats, if any, were firmly in the past.

'And what about Marlow?' remarked Samantha. 'Isn't he crazy about you?'

'Is he?' Flame felt her fists clench. 'If it had simply been a question of flirting with another woman I might have been able to forgive him, but it was more, much more than that—— Look, Sammy,' she broke off, 'I don't want to quarrel with you. Let's agree to differ on the topic of Marlow Hudson. You're like everyone else, thoroughly taken in by the superficial charm. Well, I for one have had my eyes opened, and nothing is going to make me shut them now. I know what he's really like underneath the charm, and it would make a shark look like a family pet. How do you imagine he's been so successful in business? By means of simple charm? No, he's been ruthlessly self-seeking, and you can't deny it. But that's not all.' She leaned forward. 'Even you wouldn't try to tell me he hasn't been out with any other women while I've been away.'

'If he has he's been remarkably discreet about it.' Samantha eyed her sister levelly. Then she bit her lip and glanced away.

Flame jerked back, her breath constricted cruelly in her chest at what she suspected had flashed through Samantha's mind.

'Can you imagine what he went through after you walked out?' Samantha pointed out gently. 'He's the type who'll always be knee-deep in admirers, and you can't expect a mere man to be superhuman.'

'*I* can,' clipped Flame, rising to her feet to put an end to a conversation that was becoming intolerable. She tried to change the subject. 'Is the pool warm enough for a swim yet?' It was only March, but the sun was already hot.

'Just about,' judged Samantha, 'if you keep on the move.'

'I'll have a quick dip, then, before Mother wakes up.'

Flame went back inside and in the privacy of her room spent a moment or two looking at her reflection in the mirror. What had Marlow seen in her face that had made him gaze at her with such intensity when she arrived? Perhaps he saw a woman now, not the girl he had seduced and betrayed. A woman who could handle her emotions—and, this time, one who could handle him.

Wearing a bright pink and black bikini, she strode long-limbed and still golden-skinned from a recent winter holiday into the corridor leading to the pool, but as she passed the door into the living-room it opened with a suddenness that made her jerk to a halt. Marlow himself stood in the doorway. The shock-wave that passed between them was almost tangible.

He leaned against the door-jamb, a thin smile on his handsome face. 'That was a quick change,' he ground out. 'You were on the terrace last time I looked out.'

'Shouldn't you be working instead of looking out of windows?' replied Flame, backing away as he seemed to loom over her with a distinct air of menace.

'With you around?' His voice dropped suggestively. Then his glance began to travel slowly over her near-naked body and she felt the blush that rose so easily to her flame-haired colouring rise bit by bit over her curves in a tell-tale flood.

'Damn you, Marlow,' she said through the constriction in her throat. 'Don't try your phoney charm on me any more! I had enough of it when we were married.'

'We still are married. Surely you can't have forgotten?' he husked, not moving, but riveting her attention with the sheer power of his personality. One hand snaked out and grasped her possessively by the wrist. 'I can be a patient man when necessary, Flame. And I've been patient with you.' His voice dropped. 'I've been waiting a long time.' The way he said it was full of threat and she felt the hairs at the back of her neck stand up.

'Take your hand from around my wrist, Marlow!' she clipped, refusing to struggle. She drew herself up, but couldn't help glancing down at where his fingers curled over her flesh with such an indisputable air of ownership.

'Icy—very. Definitely not one of your former attributes!'

'You'll no doubt find a lot of my so-called former attributes changed,' she told him, relief flooding through her as he slowly released her wrist and she could step back out of the danger zone. The familiar warmth of his skin showered her with sparks of memory. 'Get this straight: I'm not the naïve little girl I once was. I have a lot to thank you for, Marlow, and growing up is one of them.'

'I don't think I want to be thanked for having a hand in the way you've turned out if this is it.' His tone was hard. 'We're going to have a talk, Flame, and the sooner the better.'

'I really have nothing to say——'

'You may not have, but I've got plenty. Wait just there.' He turned back into the living-room and before she could puzzle out what he intended he was back with a leather-bound planner. 'You've just time to have a swim and change into something less likely to make me lose control,' he rasped, consulting the book. 'I've got a couple of urgent calls to make and a meeting later this morning. I'll fit you in between those. Pity I didn't know exactly when you were coming back—I'd have kept the day free. Come to my office at the *casita* in half an hour.' He snapped the book shut and gave her a look. 'Don't try to avoid it,' he ground out, correctly interpreting the mutinous expression on her face. 'I would hate to have to come and fetch you in front of everyone.'

With that he swivelled and went striding off towards the front door. Red with rage, Flame stalked outside. Ignoring Samantha, she dived into the pool, and only after a couple of lengths did she feel she'd cooled down sufficiently to emerge.

'I'm not going to mention him again, Sammy,' she said as she dried herself when she climbed out, 'but does that man make a habit of charging about the villa as if he owns it?'

'I did try to warn you. He really is one of the family now. Mother has come to rely on him more and more. And because he still lives in the *casita* we see a lot of him. I fully expected him at breakfast as usual, but maybe he decided to give us time to be alone first.'

'I can't understand why he didn't go back to his bachelor apartment when we broke up,' Flame said irritably, ignoring the hint that Marlow could show any delicacy of feeling. 'Why hang around here?'

Samantha gazed at her for a moment, then shook her head. 'Honestly, Flame, it's obvious, isn't it?'

'Is it?' Flame refused to make the inference and felt her heart harden. She knew why he'd stayed.

But Samantha wouldn't let the matter drop. 'He's always expected you to come back where you belong.'

'With that sort of confidence it must have been a shock for him to find somebody actually walking out on him. And anyway,' Flame went on as Samantha tried to re-monstrate, 'I said I didn't want to talk about him, and I meant it. There are far more important things on my mind at present. Do you think Mother's awake yet?'

'Nurse came out while you were in the pool. You can go in when you're ready. But, Flame——' Samantha looked anxious '—don't make her worry. She wants to see you both back together again. It's what she lives for now.'

With Samantha's warning in her ears and the meeting with Marlow firmly pushed to the back of her mind where she felt it belonged, Flame at last went in to see her mother. She looked as frail as she had seemed earlier when she was asleep, but though she was obviously ill her blue eyes lit up when Flame appeared in the doorway.

'Darling, they said you were coming. This is wonderful...' Her voice was a mere whisper, but she still managed to give Flame a searching glance. 'You're a lovely pale gold colour—it suits you. But aren't you rather thin, darling?'

'You sound just like your old self, Mother!' Flame searched her face for signs of illness. With a light touch of make-up Sybilla could have fooled anyone who didn't know her well. Flame sat down on the edge of the bed.

'Well?' She took Flame's hand. 'Have you come back to him or not?'

'I came back to see you. Sammy said you hadn't been feeling well——'

'Nonsense—it was absolutely nothing. I shall be as right as rain before long. I just wish I could stop worrying about you and Marlow.'

'I didn't come back with the idea of our getting back together,' Flame said carefully, Samantha's warning still ringing in her ears.

'I see.' Sybilla looked disappointed but tried to hide it. 'You must do what you feel is best, of course. But I thought by now you would have seen the error of walking out on him. He's been so patient with you...and I don't imagine patience comes easily to a man like him.'

'He's had no need to be patient. I told him it was over eighteen months ago. If he's been patient, as you call it, there must be some other reason. It's certainly not because he wants me!' As soon as she spoke Flame knew she had said the wrong thing. Her mother's eyes filled with tears.

Blinking, she asked, 'Wait until you see him. He always calls to see me before he goes to work.'

'I saw him.' Knowing she had disappointed her mother, Flame couldn't meet her eye.

'Didn't he say anything to you?'

Straight back to the point, thought Flame, feeling nettled. 'We're having a bit of a talk later,' she admitted grudgingly, hoping it wouldn't raise her mother's hopes too much. 'He's put me down in his timetable.'

'That's Marlow! He's a real dynamo.'

'He always was.'

'More so now. Your villa is finished and the hotel complex is due to open soon. Did he tell you? It was a mere sketch on his drawing-board when you left.'

'Good for him!' Flame heard the resentment in her voice and tried to give a little laugh, but her mother squeezed her hand.

'It's time, darling, it really is.'

'Time?' Flame tried to pretend she didn't know what her mother was driving at.

'Time to kiss and make up. He's looked after us all so well while you've been away. He's the son your father always wanted. Before he died he said to me, ''Sybilla, there's one thing I regret—I wish I could have given you a son to care for you when I've gone''. I told him not to be so morbid, the silly love. But if he could see Marlow now he'd know his dearest wish had come true. Emilio's a darling, but not in the same league as Marlow.' She sighed and her eyes closed, and with a jolt Flame realised what an effort it had been for her mother to keep up her usual flow of words. Her vivacity was a pretence.

The nurse popped her head round the door and diplomatically motioned for Flame to leave. She accompanied her into the corridor outside.

'How ill is she?' Flame turned puzzled eyes to her. 'She looks thinner, but——'

'She had a mild heart attack after Christmas, then on top of that she picked up some sort of virus. It's really taken it out of her. But she's a fighter. She's making progress. The trouble is she worries, doesn't she?' The nurse's face was full of sympathy and Flame felt a sudden shudder as she foresaw the consequences of the situation.

Feeling obscurely guilty, she made her way over to the *casita*.

A path ran round the side of the two-storey building, and, through the window in what had once been earmarked as their living-room because of the view, Flame saw Marlow behind a large black desk. He was on the phone with a calculator in one hand, running figures off as he spoke. He looked very much the hot property developer, the man at the top.

The marriage had been over so quickly they hadn't even had time to choose any furniture. Fortunate, she thought, as she looked round now at all the high-tech communications stuff filling the place.

'You've really taken over here, haven't you?' she remarked acidly as she stepped inside.

'Somebody has to look after the Montrose clan,' he came back without smiling.

'What's wrong with Emilio? Or Sammy, come to that? She's a fully fledged adult.'

He gave a derisive laugh. 'Much as I love those two, they're as helpless as kittens when it comes to dealing with the scale of things at Santa Margarita.'

'Whereas you know every scam going.'

His lips tightened. 'Sit down.'

'I'll stand.'

Marlow waved a hand as if he couldn't care less. 'I asked you down here so we could talk seriously about what we're going to do.'

'I thought you knew.'

He raised two dark eyebrows.

Flame's voice didn't waver. 'I want a divorce.'

'You do—I don't.'

'Oh, come on, Marlow!' she exploded. 'What possible reason could you have for wanting to hang on to a marriage like ours? A marriage in name only.'

'I don't intend it to be in name only any longer.'

'What on earth do you mean?' She eyed him in astonishment.

'I would have thought it was obvious to the most obtuse of us.'

Flame's senses lurched as she realised what he was saying. The memory of his betrayal came back like a kick in the stomach, her imagination conjuring up the image of the man she loved with another woman in his arms.

'Nothing's going to change between us,' she bit out. 'That much should be obvious even to you. And besides, you got all you really married me for the day I signed the marriage contract. Since then,' she added as coldly as she could, 'you've obviously taken steps to ensure the complete loyalty of the rest of the clan. Game and set to you, Marlow. But it doesn't mean I have to take any further part in your empire building and give you the match as well.'

'Just what are you getting at, Flame?' He sat back, steepling his fingers.

'I would have thought that was obvious to the most obtuse of us!' she riposted with a toss of her head. Her triumph was short-lived.

'You say you've grown up.' He shook his head. 'You may have acquired a little more sexual expertise while you've been in London, though even that remains to be seen, but, believe me, your growing up begins and ends there. You're still the immature girl I married. Let's try to be adult and discuss the matter properly.' He gave a perceptible sigh. 'I can't believe you're serious about what you've just been saying. Empire-building? You're not really trying to tell me you've been going around with stuff like that in your head since you left?'

His eyes seemed almost indigo. With the window behind him and his face in shadow Flame couldn't see their expression properly, but she could detect a note of incredulity in his voice. It didn't sound fake, but obviously it must be. He was still a brilliant actor. Despite her opinion, she felt her glance dwell too long on the pattern of light and shade in his face, trying to read what it meant.

Her silence must have gone on too long, for he thrust out one deeply tanned wrist to consult a watch, then his fingers began to drum impatiently as if he was waiting for an answer. It was a hand that was painfully familiar, one that had held her, caressed her, drawn cries of what now seemed like a satanic pleasure from deep within her.

Brushing her own hand rapidly across her forehead, she walked across the room to the balcony and stood gazing down into the garden. 'I should have known you'd try to talk me into something—but I would never have guessed it'd be that farrago of a marriage!' She turned. 'No doubt you have some subtle reason unbeknown to us lesser mortals. You always enjoyed these Machiavellian schemes, didn't you? That's what got you where you are today. Unluckily for you I'm no longer stupid enough not to see when I'm being used to further your ends. This is all you wanted to talk to me about, is it?' She half turned to the door. But he rose at once, stopping her in her tracks.

'*All?*' His face had darkened. 'I didn't take you lightly as my bride, Flame. And I'm not going to allow you to go on making a mockery of our marriage. You've been running around long enough. You've had your freedom. But now I'm blowing the whistle on you. You're not a child bride any longer. It's time to grow up and accept your responsibilities. I need my wife beside me—unfortunately it happens to be you!'

'How dare you, you insufferable devil? *You're* blowing the whistle? I'd like to know how! I came back here of my own free will. I wasn't waiting for *you* to give me permission!'

'I thought you came back when Samantha suggested you should,' he remarked blandly. 'Who do you think advised her to put it to you?' He gave a soft laugh. 'If you'd ignored the request I should simply have had to fly out and haul you back myself.'

'Am I hearing this?' Flame burst out.

'You're hearing me.' He gave a humourless smile. 'You must admit I've let you have a good run for your money. God knows why I should have been so reasonable. But even my patience has its limits. I want a wife now, a woman, not a child, and you're nearly twenty-one now—quite old enough to be expected to behave like an adult.'

The ferocious intensity with which he spoke made her falter, but she forced herself to face up to him. 'You don't want *me*, Marlow! You never did! Why make two of us unhappy?' Her eyes blazed. 'Can't you bear the idea of defeat?'

'Defeat, my dear *wife*, doesn't come into it. Real life isn't that sort of contest. If it were, there would be no doubt who would win. But there are much more important issues at stake.'

'Like what? Male pride? Ego? Power mania?' Her voice rose. 'There can't be anything else!'

Marlow's face was deathly pale and when he spoke his voice was like gravel. 'What about the happiness of others? To take one example, have you considered the effect all this is having on your mother?'

Flame gave a sharp intake of breath, then, collecting her wits, she threw her head back and laughed in his face. 'Really, Marlow, is that the best you can do?'

He was silent for a moment, forcing her to give him a searching glance that encompassed the austerity of his expression. 'You've seen how ill she is,' he went on with inexorable gravity. 'Her nurse will corroborate what I'm telling you. Your mother didn't get into this state overnight; it's been building since you ran away. Even you know how important our marriage is to her. All she desires is to see us together again.'

'It beats me why,' she muttered.

'Maybe she wants to feel you have someone to look after you?'

'Look after me? Like how, for instance? I can look after myself, thank you!'

'You weren't slow to cash your allowance each month,' he remarked drily.

'What the hell's my allowance got to do with you, you interfering devil? Who the hell do you think you are, prying into my private financial affairs? How dare you?'

He began to laugh softly but without much evidence of humour. 'Your financial affairs?' he mocked.

'Naturally I can't match you! You've been money-grubbing for years! But if you really want to know, I actually managed quite well in London. I had a damned good job, I'll have you know! So there! And if I did use the allowance Mother sent me on a few clothes, so what? It was *my* money—*Montrose* money!'

'Indeed?' Marlow gave a thin smile.

Brushing aside the import of what he was suggesting, Flame glowered back, rushing on to say, 'As for needing anybody, especially a predator like you!' she spat. 'Poor Mother hasn't quite caught up with the twentieth century if she thinks I need a man at any price. And anyway,' she added, 'if it comes down to that, I've already got a man.' She lifted her chin. 'He happens to be a human being, not a lying double-crosser like you. *That's* the difference!' Her thoughts had flown to Johnny and she wondered if he would mind being used in a marital battleground. Probably not!

Marlow lifted his head. Ignoring the insult, he said harshly, 'You've got a man? A lover, you mean? In London?' He paused. 'You mean someone in London?' He repeated the question as if not sure he understood what she was telling him.

Flame turned away. Her hands were shaking. When she dared look at him again, he still had that stunned look on his face that had made her avert her eyes. She'd certainly given him something to think about!

'You haven't mentioned anyone special to Samantha,' he stated swiftly without expression. 'You'd have told her if there was anyone important.'

'What on earth's it got to do with *you* whether I have a lover? When I walked out on you, Marlow, I became a free agent. You didn't imagine I wanted to spend my life hanging around here waiting for a glance from you, did you? I needed freedom.' Flame bit her lip and turned away with a lump in her heart. The only freedom she had ever wanted had been the freedom to love Marlow forever. She'd been so naïve!

'Actually I'm sure I must have mentioned him once or twice to Sam,' she blurted before she could stop herself. Put that way it sounded like the casual relationship it really was. Pulling herself together, she went on, 'I can't imagine why you're so sure she tells *you* everything. Your power isn't total, is it?' Disconcerted by his sudden stillness, she added, 'I may not have mentioned him because—because... Hell, what has my private life got to do with you any more? You forfeited the right to have any say eighteen months ago!' Suddenly unable to bear the look on his face, she crossed to the door.

'Wait!' He didn't raise his voice, but the note of command was enough to make her pause. 'Let's get one thing clear, Flame. I'm not letting you go without a fight. I don't know anything about your London lover, but as far as I'm concerned you're my wife, and I'll do everything in my power to make you remain so——— '

'Merely in order to please your mother-in-law?' she broke in scathingly.

'Obviously not. Though I'd like to please her—she's a lovely woman. But there are other considerations to be taken into account, not least the fact that you're my *wife*. You belong to *me*. I want what's mine.' His voice shook and he came round the edge of his desk towards her, every line of his face sharply etched with the intensity of his anger. 'You're back on *my* territory now, Flame. And you're going to know it.'

She trembled and stepped back, but she was determined to outface him. 'What you *want*, Marlow, and what you *get*, are often two entirely different things. To accept that as true is what *I* call maturity. You can make our divorce as difficult as you like, but get one thing straight: I'll never be anything but a wife in name. Is that what you want? Is that what you'd truly settle for?'

'Don't you believe it.' His voice was hoarse with emotion. 'I'm going to have you back, Flame. I'm going to have you body and soul. You owe me. And I want what's mine.'

As if to emphasise what he meant he reached out with one hand and let his fingers skim her body from shoulder to hip. She discovered she was breathing with sudden short, rapid breaths, her glance riveted to his face. The blue eyes flashed with recognition as he saw her reaction.

'Some things never change, and your weakness is one of them,' he murmured in a voice like silk.

'My weakness?' she managed to gasp.

'Your hunger, Flame. The one you can satisfy in no other way.'

'I don't know what you mean,' she muttered.

'I think you do. Look.' Then slowly, as if he had taken control over her will itself, Marlow placed each hand against the wall on either side of her head and without touching her in any other way brought his lips down in a kiss of tormenting slowness.

She could feel his lips, the ones she used to long for, cry for, pray for, pressure sweetly against her own, parting and probing, until her mouth began to open hungrily, irrevocably, to his. All the longing she had bottled up exploded in a spasm of wild need that shot through her with the sharpness of physical pain. It was unbidden, unwanted, and even while she was madly trying to gather her scattered forces of resistance Marlow lifted his head as smoothly as he had brought it down. There was a masked look on his face.

'There,' he murmured. 'That's your weakness. Me.' For a split second he looked as if he was about to add something else, but, apparently thinking better of it, he stepped back, pushing the door open with one hand and moving to let her leave.

Like a sleep-walker Flame groped her way outside without speaking, and only when she was safely beside the front door did she turn to look back. He stood in the doorway, a smile of unashamed triumph on his face. Then he turned and went back inside his office and closed the door. She gazed unseeingly straight ahead as she tried to bring her teeming thoughts under control.

When she had discovered Marlow was having an affair with another woman her world had crashed around her. And rather than stay to suffer the hell of living with him any longer, she had impetuously taken the first flight out, feeling instinctively that time and distance might eventually heal the wounds. Then she had gone through hell. Months when she had scarcely been able to recognise herself. But she had managed to drag herself away from the abyss and had slowly begun to pick up the pieces of her shattered existence once again.

Until Samantha had asked her to return she had really believed she was over Marlow. The shell she had built around herself had remained intact all that time. Nothing had tested it.

But now all it had taken was one look, one touch, one kiss for her defences to be smashed to smithereens. He was her first love. Yet she knew he had used her once, and whatever his reasons was now prepared to do the same again. He was a man who told lies in a voice like velvet, a man as slippery as snake oil. To her everlasting agony, he was also her husband.

CHAPTER THREE

FLAME made her way shakily towards the terrace. Her entire body seemed to be on fire, nerve-endings juddering like a crash victim's, sight blurred, hands clenching and unclenching until she forced herself to take several deep breaths and consciously relax her adrenalin-flooded limbs.

She was poised for either fight or flight, she realised, observing the physical signs, and it was all because Marlow had taken her by surprise. If she had guessed he was going to try his old tricks again, she would have been ready to resist. But he had lulled her into thinking they were to have a serious discussion about their divorce—not a reopening of the question of marriage.

What he had just said had steamrollered her into responding despite her real feelings. Now she was struggling to clamber out of the emotional wreckage.

She began to shake as she remembered his look when he informed her that he didn't want a marriage in name only. How could he contemplate long nights of loveless sex? She supposed it would be easy for him. His heated animal instinct to physically satisfy himself was all-important. Finer feelings seemed to have been honed out of existence. And he seemed to imagine she felt the same way!

Her jaw clenched and her teeth bit painfully into her lower lip as she imagined nights like that. But total confusion raged, for hadn't she herself had similar fleeting thoughts—that although she felt nothing for Marlow as a person, thinking of him as a lover she was still driven by the same insatiable need?

It was horrible. She felt trapped. She couldn't indulge her yearning to escape from the danger again, but neither did she know how to fight it. Fight him. Fight the enemy within herself—the serpent of desire that had sprung to life so suddenly once more.

Affecting an air of nonchalance with the greatest difficulty, Flame managed to settle herself on one of the black and white loungers beside the pool, remarking to Samantha as she closed her eyes, 'I'm quite tired after that night flight.'

She felt Samantha hovering nearby, no doubt wondering if she and Marlow had started to patch things up, but she resolutely kept her eyes shut until she heard the car drive off. Samantha was going to the hairdresser's and the children had already gone out with Britt. As soon as she was alone she sat up, her mind in such turmoil she couldn't keep still. She walked agitatedly beside the pool for a minute or two, thoughts and feelings teeming madly without any pattern.

Was it true what Marlow had told her—that her mother's illness was due in part to worry about their break-up? Guilt was a horrible burden to bear. But of course he would say that, wouldn't he? He had reasons of his own to make her feel bad—to put her in the wrong when it was really he himself who was the guilty party.

She trailed about the garden in a confusion of half-formed fears, but underneath it all was the searing memory of Marlow's lips covering her own. She still felt the old desire for him—that much was blatantly obvious. There was no escaping that. But how could she feel desire for such a rat? Hadn't she learned her lesson long ago? It wasn't as if there was any doubt what sort of man he was. He was as cold-blooded as a rattlesnake when it came to building up his fortune—even if cold was the last thing he was in bed.

Outside the bedroom he was a snake. A rat. An arch-manipulator of other people. An out-and-out user. But why did she always have this sneaking desire to give him the benefit of the doubt? It wasn't as if he was different when it came to personal relationships. She had caught him red-handed, another woman in his bed. What more proof did she need to have to see him in his true colours?

She had been a bride of only three weeks, and his betrayal had inflicted the pain of a physical wound. Time had healed the lacerations, but it hadn't healed the emotional scars.

Her mind flew back to that day when she had innocently made the decision to go out to Ibiza to be with her new husband. The anticipation with which she had taken a taxi from the airport, the excitement that had welled up inside her as she walked jauntily into the hotel foyer—it all came back to her now. She had been so sure of her welcome, so sure of the love with which he would greet her.

Instead, her entire world had come crashing down within seconds.

Yet even now, after all this time, just because his lips could promise such heaven, she had briefly allowed herself to consider falling in with his plans! As if she could ever contemplate going back to him! It was fright-

ening to discover that he still exerted the same old ir-
resistible magnetism.

She sat on the edge of the pool and gazed unseeingly
into the water. Her reflection was broken into a thousand
fragments by a ruffle of wind that touched the surface.
At this moment she felt her life was like that, broken
into a thousand pieces—and there seemed no way of ever
putting it together again.

A footfall behind her made her pivot, and the cold
caress of fear brought a gasp to her lips. 'How long have
you been standing there?' she croaked before she could
stop herself.

'Long enough to check you out. You're looking good.
You've lost your puppy fat.'

'Keep your opinions to yourself!' she blurted. 'Do you
think I care a damn what you think?'

'Don't you, Flame? Don't you care a damn?' His
expression was enigmatic. He was like a cat playing with
a mouse, watching her face with a cruel intensity.

'I stopped caring about you a long time ago,' she hit
out with a dismissive toss of her long hair.

'If that's true,' he said laconically, 'there's only one
thing for it—I'm going to have to make you care...all
over again.'

Flame gave a scathing laugh. 'You're going to have
your time cut out! I'd save it for something more productive if I were you!'

'My time is always productive,' he remarked, moving
slowly towards her now he'd gauged her mood. He
strolled to within a couple of feet of her, then stopped.

Like someone mesmerised against their will she tried
to tear her glance away from his, but he was looking

down at her with that cold, scrutinising expression that effectively controlled her impulses. It chilled her to have his eyes boring into hers with no sign of love in them, yet she felt herself drowning in his glance and like a drowning person reaching out, pleading, begging, the need to be plucked into the safety of his arms freezing all other emotions. She forced her glance away before he could comment on it and said, 'You make me sick! What right do you have to make me do anything?'

'The right of law,' he pointed out at once.

She raised an eyebrow, looking composed though her heart was bumping madly. 'I didn't realise you bothered about that sort of thing.' Her voice was acidic with contempt.

'When it comes down to it, darling...' his voice was like a caress '...I would dispense with every law in the land to get you where I want you.'

'I don't doubt it.' Her heart gave a flutter of fear. 'Anything to prove you're top dog, Marlow!'

Her words got through, because he lunged forward and grabbed a bunch of hair at the nape of her neck, forcing her head back so that she had no choice but to look up at him. He was bending over her, his face only inches from her own. Even then she managed to close her eyes so he couldn't see what was in them.

'I don't have to prove a damn thing, least of all to you,' he ground out. 'I get what I want when I want it. And right now what I want happens to be *you*.' He bent her head a little further back until her spine arched, but she refused to give him the satisfaction of making a complaint.

'I thought you said you wouldn't——' She bit her lip to stifle what she had been about to say and her eyes darted a glance at him in confusion.

'Wouldn't what?' he pursued. 'Wouldn't take you, perhaps?'

She lowered her eyelids, cheeks already blazing at the blatant image his words conjured up.

'I'll take you if I want to,' he intoned. 'And I'll take you when and how I want. Don't imagine you have a choice—you lost all rights to a choice when you broke the rules by running out on me.' He tightened his grip. 'You're making a big mistake if you think you can thwart me by refusing to co-operate.' His fingers were biting into the back of her head, but she refused to make a murmur.

His gaze swept her stony expression and his jaw tightened. 'I'm in no hurry to satisfy you, Flame. You can wait for it. I've got time on my side. I know I'm going to get you in the end—on my terms.'

'Not a chance,' she managed to croak. 'I'll never give in!'

'Tell yourself that if it helps, but it'll get you precisely nowhere. Unfortunately for you you've reached the end of the line. There's nowhere else for you to run.'

'I'll go back to England,' she sparked, trying not to let him see how ragingly humiliated she felt to be pinned so helplessly in his grip. It only compounded the humiliation to hear what he said.

Still sitting on the edge of the pool with her feet in the water, she couldn't even begin to wriggle free while Marlow stood over her like her lord and master. Inside she cringed with shame, but instead of showing it she tried to flick the long tendrils of amber hair away from her face with a gesture of disdain, while pretending he didn't have her trapped at all.

He greeted her words with a tight smile and informed her, 'You're not going to England or anywhere if I don't say so, baby. I thought you'd guessed that much by now.'

'You can't stop me!' she hissed, trying not to struggle.

'No?' He laughed openly and her eyes dwelled too long on the features that made him look as handsome as the devil, so that triumph lurked in his eyes as soon as he saw it. He leaned over her. 'I can stop you doing whatever I want. You forget, you're on my territory now. And if you want to put me to the test, make your move. Let's see how you make out.'

'If I want to, Marlow,' she said with as much hauteur as she could muster, 'I can walk out of this villa right now. I've got my passport, I've got money. There's no way you could stop me.'

'I've always regarded physical restraint as a crude last resort,' he remarked. 'Surely we're not going to sink to that level?'

'Then what do you mean?' Flame whipped back.

'You're still here,' he pointed out.

'Nothing to do with you, so don't flatter yourself!' she retorted.

'No? But it was I who pointed out the consequences if you suddenly took off again,' he observed almost mildly. 'Surely you're not forgetting your obligations to your mother?'

'You think you've trapped me by resorting to emotional blackmail? But it was nothing to do with you and what you wanted that brought me back,' she managed to return. 'If it wasn't for Mother I wouldn't have come back at all.'

'You would if I'd *wanted* you back.'

She gave a small gasp and turned her head. Even now he could wound her with the knowledge of his deeper emotional indifference to her. Did he already know how it had seared her to the soul to know that he hadn't at any point asked her to return?

'If you didn't want me back at any time in the last eighteen months,' she gritted, 'I don't see why you should pretend to want me back now.'

'But you've got it wrong, Flame.' His voice dropped to a seductive deeper level. 'I'm not *pretending* to want you back. I do want you—passionately.' His eyes lazed over her upturned face, noting how helplessly she was arched beneath him. 'I've already told you,' he went on throatily, 'my patience is now over. I'm calling in the debt. You've owed me for too long. And now you're going to repay what you've withheld—with interest!'

'It always comes back to money, doesn't it? You can't think of anything without reference to profit and loss!' Her eyes blazed with contempt.

Marlow laughed softly. 'You would say that, obviously, because it's a part of your own game.'

'What on earth do you mean?' she exclaimed.

'You know that when you come to inherit you're going to be a very rich young woman in your own right should you choose to sell Cabo Margarita. Maybe now you've tasted freedom you feel you don't want to share your wealth with anything so inconvenient as a husband?' His lips twisted. 'Tough luck, lady—you've got me to contend with and you're not going to forget it!'

Confused, Flame tried to jerk her head away. 'You're hurting my neck,' she muttered. What he had just said had never occurred to her.

In answer to her protest, his fingers tightened convulsively. 'Hurting it? I ought to break it,' he breathed, drawing her closer beneath him. When she flinched he went on, 'I see you have no answer for me. You must really hate me for spoiling your little scheme! How inconvenient for you that you made that disastrous decision to marry at the age of nineteen—though even you must admit you were eager at the time.'

'Damn you to hell, Marlow. I hate you!'

'Oh, I know that,' he murmured in a caressing tone. 'I've grown used to that idea. It no longer enters into my calculations. I may even hate you too. But so what? There are more things in life than love. Like sex, for instance. And we both know we're in accord on *that* one!'

'You might think so, but I've got news for you,' she managed to say, her heart racketing painfully as his words lashed her like silken whips. 'I don't go to bed with anybody out of blind lust. I have to care completely——'

'You must have changed a hell of a lot,' he broke in harshly. 'I seem to remember you couldn't get enough of me in the old days. Even you wouldn't try to convince me that you wanted anything but my body then, would you?' His fingers raked her scalp. *'Would you?'* he demanded.

'If you say so.' She lowered her eyelids at the thought that he had never known how much she had really cared.

'So where have all these finer feelings come from?' he rasped. 'If indeed they exist anywhere but in your imagination.'

'Maybe people change,' she fought back, risking a glance at him. 'Maybe they learn that there's more to life than possessing someone——'

'Or being possessed?' murmured Marlow with a tilt of his eyebrows. His voice had thickened. 'We're wasting time, darling. We both know it. Instead of talking we could be pleasuring each other in the only way we both understand... Quit this talk about finer feelings, it won't wash. These last months have shown me how you really are.'

Flame wondered what he was going to do next, but his words left her in no doubt. 'Let's get down to business,' he muttered hoarsely against the side of her head.

'Don't, Marlow!' The cry was torn from her lips as she suddenly found herself sinking back beneath his weight on to the mosaic tiles beside the pool. Her feet still trailed in the water and one of his knees placed between her thighs effectively prevented her from struggling free. *'Don't!'* she began again, more strongly.

She moved her head violently from side to side as she guessed what was coming next. Sure enough, his free hand came up and gripped her chin, then his mouth covered her own in the heat of possession, prising open her lips to allow her tongue its invasion. She felt herself weaken under the force of his suddenly unleashed desire, and the more rapidly she breathed, the more passionate his response. Soon she couldn't tell whether her panting came from the exertion of trying to resist or from the desire that ripped through her loins in response to his own. A small sound of surrender was torn from her throat as his mouth lifted at last. He noticed it with satisfaction.

'We're good together when we don't talk,' he observed. 'Why don't we always keep things this simple?'

'Because real life isn't simple!' she bit back, wriggling sideways to get away.

'Do that some more,' he muttered against the side of her cheek. Flame didn't have to ask what he meant. Her ineffectual squirming had brought her achingly up close beneath him and she could feel the hard male response burning between her thighs as a blatant sign of his desire. His lips were already consuming the rest of her resistance, feasting on the sweetness of her curves with an insatiable appetite, and when his dark head of tangled hair lifted to search out other places of delight she felt the outside world slip beyond consciousness with the final surrendering thought that at least they were shielded from prying eyes by the huge poolside parasol.

His experienced touch made her open like a flower long deprived of rain, forcing her to groan his name in a helpless submission, all resistance to him impossible so long as his touch plundered her senses like this. He had said he would take her when and how he wanted, and now he was giving her the proof.

But there was another side of the coin, as he had warned. When she was on the verge of begging him to take her, her fingers raking helplessly up and down the broad, curving muscles of his back, Marlow shifted his weight, and when she opened her eyes he had propped himself over her with a hand on each side of her head, gazing down at her with the shuttered look she had seen before.

As she watched he moved back, slowly dragging himself to one side, then, while she was still trying to fathom what he was doing, he rose athletically to his feet in one sudden movement. 'Is it luck or what that I have a phone call to take in five minutes?' His lips twisted into a derisive smile. 'Do you still imagine you're calling the shots? I told you you'd have to wait, Flame. I'll decide when,' he informed her disparagingly. 'But don't worry, it won't be long.'

He seemed to expect her to argue with him, but she felt too shocked, too bleared by his abrupt withdrawal to think straight. In a daze she watched him begin to walk away. It was in her mind to call after him, but she fought back the impulse, suddenly aware of her surroundings, of what had been about to happen, of her own shameless, helpless part in the proceedings. My God, what am I doing? she thought frantically, pulling her top down over her midriff. Marlow was already at the steps leading round the side of the villa. Let him go, Flame admonished herself breathlessly. It was agony to force back the cry of longing that welled up in her throat.

Tears released by the depth of her frustration and despair sprang into her eyes. Why was he taunting her like this?

When he had gone, without, she noticed with a twinge, a single backward glance, she sat up and tried to steady herself. It was a bleak fact that she would never survive life with Marlow. He wanted too much and he would give nothing that really mattered. Only a fool would have contemplated opening themselves to the degree of pain he could inflict.

She got up and went towards the villa, not entirely sure what she was doing. Her mind was in turmoil, unsatisfied desire like a tornado of flame deep within. She stood on the steps for an extended moment, gazing unseeingly at the bright disc of the swimming-pool.

At last she turned towards the house again. There was a movement on her mother's balcony, then the nurse came out. She leaned down. 'Would you like to come up?' she called.

Wordlessly Flame made her way inside. She felt like a zombie with the strain of trying to wipe all signs of emotional turmoil from off her features. A pause and a deep breath before she entered the sick-room gave her a semblance of control.

But she was even more disturbed when she went inside and saw how ill her mother looked. The fine skin stretched across her cheekbones seemed almost transparent. 'Is there anything I can get you, Mum?' she asked gently, managing to shelve her own problems for the time being.

'Nurse Gomez is taking her break. I hoped we might have a little chat.' Sybilla smiled weakly. Lifting a hand, she indicated the photographs on the table beside her bed. 'Aren't they beautiful children?' she breathed. 'I'm so lucky.'

Flame picked up the photographs of her little nieces and nephew. 'I couldn't believe they'd grown so much when I saw them,' she said rather pensively. 'They were only babies eighteen months ago.' A twinge of regret crept into her voice as she contemplated the three cute little faces, all smiles and dancing eyes and baby chubbiness.

'I love listening to them playing on the terrace,' her mother went on. 'They're like little larks, as happy as the day is long.' She gave a scarcely perceptible sigh, then said something that sent a stab of pain straight through Flame's heart. 'If only you and Marlow had a baby,' she said, 'I'm sure things would sort themselves out. And just think, they'd all be of an age. It would be such fun for them, growing up together.' Her faded blue eyes brightened at the thought.

'Mother, I don't think——'

'I know Marlow wants a family. Someone to hand it all on to——'

'Mother, is this what you wanted to chat about, because if so——?'

'Of course it is, my darling,' Sybilla went on in a voice that was no more than a whisper. 'What else is more important than my own daughter's happiness? I hate to see you waste your life being miserable——'

'Who's miserable?' Flame tried to laugh it off, but something in the remark struck home, making her eyes mist over. She averted her head, pretending to put the photographs back in place. There was silence from her mother and when she turned Sybilla had struggled up on to her pillows, not hiding the depth of her concern.

'I've grown very fond of Marlow over this last year,' she admitted, her voice wavering. 'He's been absolutely staunch. You've got a good man there, Flame, and I really wonder if you know what you're doing to him.'

'What *I'm* doing to *him*?' Flame gazed in open-mouthed astonishment. Then, seeing the look of pain on her mother's face, she clamped her lips over the angry words that were about to come pouring out. Her mother's face seemed almost waxen now against the lace pillows, and not for the first time Flame got an inkling of just how ill she was. The hand on the coverlet was so fragile it wrenched her heart.

She said, 'We had a bit of a talk before he went out...' It was said in a way meant to allay her mother's acute anxiety, but Sybilla Montrose read more into it than Flame intended.

'There now,' she sighed, 'that's a beginning! I knew you only needed to meet again. I'm not expecting miracles—I know you're both stubborn. But I can't forget your faces as you stood side by side at the altar. You were two people in love if ever there were.' She smiled. 'I would never have agreed to such a whirlwind marriage if I hadn't felt convinced you were both so absolutely right for each other. And I don't just mean the money side,' she said, with a flash of her old shrewdness before Flame could interrupt. 'Love should transcend all that.'

'And you believe it did?' mumbled Flame, letting her hair fall forward to hide the expression on her face.

'I know it did,' came the reply. Still wan-faced, Sybilla stretched out an arm. 'Darling, would you do something for me? Open that drawer in my dressing-table—the one on the left. Yes, that's right,' she added as Flame rose to do her bidding.

As she pulled the drawer open Flame understood what was expected of her. Inside lay a photograph in a silver frame. It was the one taken outside the church on that distant summer's day when she had stood beside Marlow, her hand tucked trustingly in his. Her own face was radiant with innocent happiness, and Marlow looked straight out at the camera with what Flame now read as smug satisfaction.

The memory seared her when she recalled how, after the photograph had been taken, Marlow had bent to kiss her as little paper hearts and flowers whirled enchantingly about their heads.

'You're mine now,' he had whispered, 'forever, my lovely.' At the time it had made her feel safe, protected. Now it seemed like a sentence in hell.

Her fingers closed over the edge of the frame and she handed it silently to her mother, then watched as it was placed carefully beside the rest of the photographs on the bedside table. Her mother's next words confirmed her fears. 'That's where it has always belonged,' she smiled. 'Just as you will always belong to Marlow, my darling.'

Flame knew that now was not the time to tell her the marriage was truly over. If a separation of eighteen months hadn't convinced her, nothing she said at this point would make any difference. Besides, how could she shatter the optimism of a sick woman? She made up her mind that she would have to break it to her gently over a period of time. Once Sybilla saw the truth of it she would come to accept that some things could never be, no matter how hard we wanted them.

Sybilla's eyes were closing now. 'They tell me I should sleep as much as I can, but it seems such a waste when you've only just arrived. I want to hear all about London, and there's so much to tell you too—about the garden, about Marlow's wonderful plans—though I'm sure he'll want to tell you about those himself—and Flame, most of all...' she paused as if suddenly lacking the strength to go on '...most of all,' she forced herself to continue, 'I want to tell you what a relief it is to have you home. All the details of my will have to be discussed, and I so want you here for that.'

Flame's heart gave a lurch. 'Mother, I won't hear this sort of talk! Who cares about wills, for heaven's sake? You're getting better—I know you are!' She felt her senses swim with the premonition of sudden loss. It was something she had never really considered before.

'It's important to make sure everyone gets what they want,' Sybilla continued, with an obvious effort to rally her strength. 'Marlow may own the hotels on the headland and the holiday village he's building beside the beach, but we still own the land on which they're being built. I want to see things settled properly in case anything happens... If you'd gone ahead with a divorce it could have been a tricky situation for him. Luckily, now——'

'Luckily now Marlow has nothing to worry about?'

Sybilla smiled contentedly. 'Just so, darling. It's a great load off my mind.'

Flame couldn't think of anything to say that could adequately express her feelings. Aware that her mother had already taxed her strength, she remained silent as she helped her settle down to sleep. Nurse Gomez nodded approvingly when she came in a few minutes later. 'Your arrival has been a great tonic for her,' she confided at the door, 'but we mustn't overdo things. It's still early days.'

Flame went outside when she saw she could be of no further help. Underneath her calm exterior her mind was a seething mass of fury. Hadn't she known Marlow was up to something? She gave a hollow laugh. To think she had almost surrendered yet again!

What a fool she was to think it didn't matter that Marlow was still the same self-seeking snake as ever! Still up to his old tricks—building up his empire by fair means or foul. Worming his way into the confidence of a sick woman, and now, dragging Flame herself back into the labyrinth of his ambitions when it suited him best, filling her ears with a load of lies, making everything follow the same pattern as before. What he really wanted, all along, was not a wife but the land she brought with her.

So nothing changes, nothing changes, she told herself furiously. 'I want what's mine,' he had had the gall to tell her, leading her to believe he meant her, his wife. That was bad enough, but what he had really meant was that he wanted to bed her in order to set the seal on his possession of Cabo Santa Margarita!

How could she fall for it again? How could she?

Rage surged in every fibre. To think she had secretly begun to harbour the hope that his desire might be the beginning of something else!

Eighteen months ago—she reminded herself—then, when she had been too young to know any better, she had believed what they felt for each other was true love. Now, surely, there was no excuse for succumbing to the same puerile delusion? This time around she hadn't even got the excuse that he'd given her that line. He'd been brutally honest about his finer feelings—or lack of them.

She shuddered at the thought of how easy it had been to persuade her to begin to weaken. He hadn't even had to say the little words of endearment any woman might expect. There had been no pretence at loving her this time. No gentleness. No sign of caring. Just the crude expression of primitive male desire. She blushed to think how she herself had responded to that!

She had made his job of deception so easy for him. He hadn't even had to try. Her reaction to his blatant attempt at seduction had proved how easily he could arouse her! All he'd had to do was demonstrate that she couldn't say no!

Blushing with the humiliating knowledge that she'd allowed herself to be duped again, Flame paced angrily up and down the terrace. Minus Samantha and the children the place seemed unnaturally empty. It seemed to reflect her own inner desolation as she contemplated the long days stretching ahead—for, no matter how she looked at it, one thing was clear: she couldn't walk out again. Not just yet. Not with her mother in her present state of health. She would have to shelve her own feelings and stay on until she was out of danger. She could hardly bear to imagine what it was going to be like. But she would *have* to do it, for her mother's sake.

But how would Sybilla take the obvious signs that the marriage was over? She shuddered to think. Then she forced herself to consider all the implications of remaining at Santa Margarita—trying to pretend that everything was fine... It was impossible to imagine. It would be hell on earth.

The arrival of Samantha's car in the drive put an end to such speculations. Flame went to the front to greet her.

'Ready for lunch, Flame?' Samantha emerged from the car behind an enormous bunch of flowers, adding, 'I expected to find you asleep after your flight.'

'Asleep?' Flame gave a derisive laugh. 'I should be so lucky!'

'It must be disturbing—the worry over Mother, and then Marlow.' Samantha gave her a searching glance. 'If you're still wide-eyed this evening you must have dinner with Emilio and me in town. It'll do you good to get back into the swing of things. Some friends are having a bit of a party—nothing special, though.'

'Special enough to have your hair done.' Flame walked back into the house with her.

'No, this is just my weekly do. If you want a good man I thoroughly recommend him——'

'A *good man*?' Flame couldn't help giving a scathing laugh. 'Hard to find, aren't they?'

Samantha chuckled, not detecting the stratum of pain that lay beneath Flame's flippant mood. 'I'll just pop into Mother's with these flowers if she's awake.'

Flame let her go and went to change for lunch. She wondered if Marlow would be joining them. He had a meeting, but business usually finished in time for lunch at two, followed by a siesta. That had been the pattern in the short period of bliss after the honeymoon. She refused to imagine what the word siesta had taught her to expect.

*   *   *

When Samantha emerged from the sick-room Flame was on the patio sipping a pre-lunch sherry and trying to talk herself down to normal again, but her attempt was short-lived. Samantha's face was one big, happy smile.

'Darling, I'm so pleased you're being sensible. And it seems to have done her a world of good already. She's looking better than she has for weeks!'

'Sorry?' Flame paused with the glass halfway to her lips.

Just then Emilio came roaring outside with two of the toddlers draped over his shoulders and Samantha's attention was distracted for a moment. Flame puzzled over her words, but with a distinct lowering of her spirits. What had Samantha been getting at? Patently it was to do with Marlow and her mother's expectations.

'Sammy, please——' She pulled at her sister's arm when she briefly took her eyes off her beloved offspring. 'What has Mother been saying?'

'Why, about you and Marlow, of course!' Samantha replied, confirming Flame's suspicions. 'I must say I was rather surprised after what you'd been saying earlier, but I suppose your talk with him has helped begin to clear the air a little.' She gave a wicked laugh. 'Trust you two to get on with things while we're all still dreaming and hoping! It's your courtship all over again! Talk about whirlwinds! Oh, and here he is, dynamo man himself, right on cue!'

Whether he was on cue or not, Flame couldn't be certain, but it was certainly Marlow in the flesh. She dragged her glance away before he could notice her betraying appraisal.

Blazingly conscious of his proximity, she waited until they were all seated at the table, then, taking a deep breath, she announced in a voice loud enough to penetrate even Samantha's well-meaning but rather premature assumption, 'Everybody's under the misapprehension that we're getting together again, Marlow—— '

'And aren't we?' he broke in at once. 'Surely that's what we agreed just now?' He looked at her with faked good humour, his eyes when they met hers like shards of ice, daring her to deny it.

Samantha obviously missed this silent exchange and gave a light laugh. 'You do tease, Flame! You had me worried for a minute. But I knew Mother couldn't be mistaken. She was simply too sure of herself. It would kill her if it was all a false alarm.'

Flame clutched the edge of her chair. 'I hope you don't mean that literally.'

'Whether she did or not, she's probably right,' broke in Marlow. 'It's clear how much this marriage means to her.' He gave Flame a piercing glance from beneath jet-dark brows.

She shivered involuntarily. It seemed as if her fate was being decided for her again. She felt like the helpless baby of the family once more. There were too many people in charge. But Marlow was already going on before she could bring any sort of protest to her lips.

'We thought we'd give it one more try, Samantha. We both admit we made mistakes,' he was saying with mind-boggling aplomb.

Flame's sharp intake of breath was audible. 'Wait a minute—— '

'And Flame has decided to shelve her objections in deference to her mother's wishes,' he went on, ignoring her. 'She's going to come back for six months and give it a try. If by that time it isn't working, we'll call it a day.'

'But——' Flame's mouth opened and closed like a fish out of water.

'That's an excellent idea,' Emilio, silent until now, voiced his opinion too, and Samantha chimed in in agreement. Flame could only stare stony-faced at them all.

'I'm being set up again,' she said hoarsely when she eventually found her voice. Tongues of fire seemed to run up and down her spine.

'What did you say?' It was Samantha.

'He knows!' Flame shot back, glaring straight at Marlow. Suddenly unable to bear the pressure of their stares, she scrambled to her feet. 'I can't eat!' she exclaimed. 'And if you want to know the reason why——' she glared at her sister '—ask my so-called husband. He has *all* the answers!'

She plunged off down the garden, a red tide of anger blinding her to where she was going. All she registered were Marlow's enigmatic expression and Samantha's astonished cry following after.

By the time she reached the cliff path she was safely out of sight of the house. But she kept on walking, anxious only to put as much distance as possible between herself and Marlow's smug satisfaction at the *fait accompli* he had somehow engineered.

Reaching the top, she was breathless and flung herself down on an outcrop of rock to gaze unseeingly out to sea. It was while she was sitting there that she heard a sound on the path. Turning, she saw Marlow himself, a glass of wine in each hand, making his way purposefully towards her.

'Here, you look as if you could do with one,' he said, without expression, handing her one of the glasses. 'I take it you're having second thoughts.'

'*Second?* I haven't had time to have first thoughts yet. It seems as if everything's been decided between the lot of you already!'

'I must admit I was surprised to hear Samantha announce that we were back together. I assumed you'd actually understood what I'd been saying this morning and decided to tell everybody.'

'Not a bit of it. Samantha's been talking to Mother. And Mother—well,' Flame scrubbed viciously at the path with the stub of her sandal, 'Mother managed to get hold of the wrong end of the stick this morning. Her ambition to see us together obviously got the better of her understanding.' Stifling her rage in case it got the better of her, she lifted her head and looked him in the eye. 'I really ought to congratulate you, Marlow,' she said without a tremor in her voice. 'You've got them all in the palm of your hand. How on *earth* do you manage to do it?'

'I don't know what that's supposed to mean.' He sat down beside her.

She was vibrantly conscious of the touch of his thigh against her own, and it brought a sudden sweeping remembrance of the way he had held her earlier. Even the scent of his skin seemed capable of flooding her mind with desire.

It was shattering how the mere brush of his arm against her skin could ignite such feelings, especially when she felt an all-consuming rage at the double game he was playing.

She edged away, but he turned to her, putting out a hand to grip her arm with a possessiveness that made her head swim.

'Six months—that's all. If you still feel you can't stand the sight of me by then—or I of you,' he added cruelly, 'we'll call the whole thing off and you can have your divorce.' He made it sound so eminently reasonable and, coupled with the demands of her mother's welfare and her own insatiable longing to belong to him even for as short a time as six months, Flame was almost swayed.

Then she gave him a swift, pitying look. 'Clever, Marlow. But not clever enough! You know as well as I do that given another six months without cohabiting a divorce would be the easiest thing in the world on grounds of desertion. But if we live together—well, it's going to mean I shall have to start from scratch again. Unless,' she smiled bitterly, 'you obligingly provide me with proof of adultery.'

She felt his grip on her arm tighten. 'What the hell are you suggesting? You don't imagine you'd get me on those grounds, do you?'

'You're far too clever,' she agreed coldly. 'It would always be my word against yours. And blue eyes are so convincing.' She slithered out of his grasp, and, rising to her feet, she said, 'Just because you got away with it all once before please don't imagine it's going to happen a second time. And Marlow,' she added, 'please don't bother to lie to me. It's too late. And besides, I know the real reason you want to remain married to me. Mother has just let it slip.'

'What the hell are you raving about?' rasped Marlow, standing up beside her.

She looked up at him, her eyes probing his for a sign that he was going to change tack and give her the truth, but he stuck to what he'd said.

'I don't fool as easily this time around, as you'll discover.' She glared up at him. 'I should have suspected you were up to something the first time, but I was too young to understand that some people put grabbing what they can above human feelings. I guess *love* is way down your scale of values.'

She stood looking up at him for a protracted moment, twisting the stem of the wine glass between her fingers and perversely longing for him to defend himself. 'You look so convincing sometimes, I might almost believe you, even now. Maybe you genuinely find it difficult to tell where truth ends and fiction begins,' she mocked. 'But I suspect it's a completely cold-blooded calculation—with me as the pawn yet again.' A scornful laugh was squeezed from her when he didn't defend himself. 'Really, Marlow. I'm amazed you're not rushing in with counter-arguments as usual! Though perhaps even you realise it wouldn't work this time around.'

'I don't—none of this makes sense.' He narrowed his glance. 'What's making you say all this?'

'D'you know something?' she said, ignoring his question as beneath contempt. 'I believe I would almost admire you if you could admit frankly what an utter bastard you are. There would be something almost heroic in such an admission. It's your rank hypocrisy *I* can't stand!'

With a pain like a hunk of concrete lodged in her throat Flame swung away down the cliff path without bothering to say anything else.

His position was indefensible and he knew it. Even he knew he couldn't hope to brazen his way out of the situation. That was why he was speechless now.

She was nearly at the bottom of the incline when she heard him coming down behind her. She increased her pace. Then he gained on her and she felt a hand bite into her shoulder, jerking her round to face him amid a landslide of stones.

For a moment they outstared each other like two wild animals, the tension of unexpressed rage making Marlow shake on the very edge of losing control. Then something seemed to happen. Instead of saying what he'd obviously intended to say he reached for her with a muffled groan instead, dragging her savagely against the hard-packed muscles of his body, crushing the breath out of her till she had to fight for air.

As she plunged to free herself he rasped, 'God damn you, Flame! You're a destroying creature, and I don't know what your game is, but you're not going to get away with it! Do you hear what I'm saying?'

'Let me go, Marlow! Take your lies elsewhere! I don't have to listen!' she shouted.

Her own body was beginning to tremble from head to foot to match his as she felt his will battle against her own. His voice was a caress as he felt her resistance begin to seep away, and with his familiar seductive power he murmured huskily, 'When I first met you I thought you the most innocent, delectable thing on God's earth.' The blue eyes glinted beneath short black lashes. 'But underneath that angelic exterior you're as hard as nails. It's a side of you I hadn't suspected until you walked out on me. I misjudged you——'

'You're damned right you did!' Flame felt his power flow around her and, despite the energy of her response, she had to shut her eyes to block the image of his face hovering so dangerously near her own in case it made her weaken further.

'What did you want from me, Flame, in those early days?' he murmured beside her mouth. 'I wanted to give you everything I possessed—I thought I'd made that clear enough. What more could I have given you? I laid my name, my wealth, my life, at your feet—wasn't that enough for you?'

'I suppose that was fair exchange for what you wanted in return,' mocked Flame, her heart like a stone.

'What did I want in return?'

'We all know the answer to that one!' She averted her glance. It wasn't worth stating. And naturally Marlow wouldn't understand what she had wanted. How could he when it was beyond his capabilities to imagine it? There had only ever been one thing, and it wasn't money or possessions! It was his love. That was all she had yearned for in those days. The sort of love that went hand in hand with fidelity. It was obviously a foreign concept to a man like Marlow Hudson. Her face felt like marble as she raised it. 'Don't play games with me, Marlow,' she muttered, trying to close her eyes against the laser-bright glance that was remorselessly sweeping her features. 'You know exactly what I mean!'

'I'm not playing games. Far from it,' he countered. 'I've never been more serious in my life. I want answers, Flame. What did you think I wanted?'

'You wanted blood!' she jerked out.

He gave a harsh laugh. 'There's no understanding you! So how do you see the situation now? Do I still want blood, whatever that means?'

'You know the truth as well as I do!' Flame tried to struggle out of his grasp, but he dragged her back with a sudden curse.

'I want what's mine!' he ground out.

'Yours, yours, yours!' she hissed. 'That's all you think about! Well, I'm not going to be one of your things, to be owned, to be catalogued beside all your other pieces of property! I'm a human being! I have feelings and desires that have nothing to do with *you*!' His grip tightened, but she twisted, flushed-faced, in his arms, crying, 'Why should I be filed away with all your other possessions with your name branded all over me?'

'Because I want it!' he ground out. 'You are mine, whatever you say. You gave me your promise—till death. You broke that promise. But you've still got my name. It is my brand, Flame. I gave it to you—Flame Hudson. You're mine, and you'll never be anything else!'

'I'm a Montrose!' she spat. 'And shall be until the day I die! Nothing you can do will ever come between me and my family! Not you, not your pirating of our land, not all your lawyers and your millions! Nothing can come between us! My family are first!'

Marlow's face wore a suddenly haggard look, his lips tightening in some sort of pain, but that fleeting impression of physical hurt was really anger, Flame judged, her eyes meeting his in a mutual razoring, anger that she had the temerity to stand up to him!

'You can do what you like to me,' she gritted, 'but you'll never, never own me!'

'I can and I will!' he ground out in a voice that made her flinch with its tone of menace. 'I've won tougher battles than this. A mere girl like you isn't going to stand between me and what I want!'

'Now we're getting to it,' she managed to croak triumphantly. 'We're getting to the real reason you say you want me back!'

He raised two coal-black eyebrows. 'And?'

'The land, the land—it always comes back to that.'

'Land?' He looked surprised. 'You always come back to that, it seems. I was thinking of rather more intimate desires...'

She didn't have to ask what he meant. The glitter of his eyes as they trailed over the rise and fall of her breasts told her as blatantly as the words that followed. 'How many times do I have to say it? How many different ways do you need to know? I want you—your lips, your skin, your hair, I own it all, and you're going to know it. I want it all back, Flame. I want you back, back where you belong, in my bed, naked, crying out to me in surrender as you once used to. Fight if your pride tells you you must. But in your heart, you know it's as inevitable as sunrise and sunset—you'll be back where I want you. You can't escape.'

The power of his words almost persuaded her to give in at once—he made it seem as if every exit was blocked. But the bitterness of knowing he didn't, maybe couldn't, love her made her fight back. 'You can use your dominance to force me to do some things, Marlow. But you can't force me to submit willingly. I'll never do that! Never!'

Even as she spoke he pulled her hard against him and his fingers began to measure a feverish rhythm, caressing and exploring the long mane of flame-coloured hair that so aptly mirrored her name, and as he dragged her against his ill-concealed arousal she felt her own response, despite her intentions, ignite like an insidious lick of fire deep inside.

'No, Marlow, no!' she protested as she felt her resistance crumble with the increasing intimacy of his touch.

But at the moment when she saw her control hanging by a single thread he began to release her. 'You want me,' he said harshly. 'You always did—that hasn't changed. When all the words have been said it still comes down to this.' He skimmed her peaked breasts with one hand as if to demonstrate what he meant. 'But I'm not a fool. This time the bargaining is going to be equal on both sides. I'm not going to give you the triumph of asserting your sexual dominance—I refuse to give you the satisfaction—until I get something in return.' He paused. 'You know what I want. I want you to give me your word. I want you to give me the next six months. Say it, Flame. Six months—that's all you've got to give.'

CHAPTER FOUR

FLAME had walked on after this, so Marlow wasn't going to force her to make love there and then on the cliff top! That was something to be thankful for!

Relief, tinged with another feeling she didn't want to own, mixed in confusion with her sheer anger that he was using her again. And he was so blatant about it! Six months, he had said. She wasn't that stupid. Six months would give the lawyers time to sew up all the details of who owned what—she didn't need telling it was that that was uppermost in his mind when he set a time limit on their marriage!

When she heard him come up behind her she lifted blazing eyes to his, barely able to conceal her contempt. With an effort she managed to force the shakiness out of her voice. 'You're trying to blackmail me by an appeal to my concern for my mother,' she stated flatly.

Marlow shook his head. 'Don't be ridiculous! You're a free agent—nobody's coercing you. All I'm doing is trying to point out the ramifications of pursuing your own selfish course. It's about time you started to think of other people. Your mother needs you. You need to grow up and consider what other people want for a change.'

'That's rich, coming from you!' Flame tossed her head and made off down the cliff path again. Anywhere, she thought blindly as she stumbled on, anywhere to get away from him and his hateful words. But she could hear him coming down behind her in single-minded pursuit no matter how quickly she tried to forge ahead.

If it had been possible she would have taken to her heels, but she knew there was to be no running away this time. As it was, her thoughts flew frantically this way and that in an attempt to escape the net he was tightening around her.

What if she insisted he accept the marriage as it had been over the last eighteen months? she thought frantically. He had said he was going to have more than a marriage in name, but, if he wanted to keep up the charade that it was her mother's health that was the overriding factor, surely he would have to accept whatever terms she offered? They could make things appear normal on the surface, just until her mother's health improved. Could he accept that, she wondered, or would his urge to take what he claimed was his make him refuse to listen?

She stopped abruptly on her downward flight and Marlow put out a hand to stop himself bumping into her. He left it there, resting on her arm, her wound-up senses racing at his touch again so that for a moment she almost forgot what she wanted to put to him. Then she brushed it off and gave him a weighing glance.

'It looks as if I'll have to stay—for Mother's sake. But I'll only stay on one condition...'

His glance raked her upturned face. 'Go on.'

'I'll behave as your ever-loving wife,' she dragged out, 'but...only in public.'

He jerked back as if she had struck him. 'No way!' he snarled. 'I'm calling the shots this time . . . and you'll be in my bed—every night—exactly where you belong!'

'Then that's it!' she gritted. 'I guessed you'd be too damned selfish to consider it! So much for your vaunted concern over Mother's health!'

'You mean you'll go back to England if I don't agree?' he enquired, velvet-voiced and with a cynical tilt of his head.

She hadn't thought it out as far as that, but her silence drew a mocking smile from him. 'Even you aren't as callous as that, Flame. You'll stay,' he said emphatically. 'On any terms I set. You have no choice—I think you realise that.'

When he had said he wanted to possess her the savagery of his declaration had frightened her. Yet what he was now saying seemed irrefutable. Her mother was too ill at present to cope with the trauma of their divorce.

Reluctantly she saw that it was true. She couldn't break her mother's heart, or worse—even if it meant breaking her own. 'I hate you, Marlow. I wish I'd never set eyes on you.' She spoke with such quiet venom it made his head jerk up. 'You know I can't argue with you. I can't leave Mother. You've been counting on that!' She felt tears of anger begin to course down her cheeks as the thought of the months ahead filled her imagination. 'You'll be happy—you'll get what you want,' she said emptily, referring to the consolidation of his hold over Santa Margarita, 'and Mother gets what she wants, so she'll be happy. The only one not happy is me. Well, don't worry!' her voice rose. 'I'll survive—I've had to learn how. I'll survive this, for Mother's sake. It won't be forever. She'll get better. And then—you'd better believe it—you won't see me for dust!'

Then her thoughts flew to Johnny. He was her only avenue of escape. But would he want her after this? To be honest, she didn't really care. She was already back inside her nineteen-year-old self when she had lived and breathed for Marlow. It left no room for anyone else. But this time she could see her involvement for what it was, base sexual attraction. She didn't love Marlow. How could she when she hated him so much?

By the time Marlow allowed her to walk back up towards the villa the terrace was deserted and the maid had cleared lunch. The long curtains at the bedroom windows were closed, and Flame guessed that everyone would siesta for the next couple of hours.

'Looks as if we've missed lunch. Let's go and raid the larder.' Marlow's voice lacked expression and she knew what she had told him was still on his mind.

'Just deal straight with me!' she exploded as he brushed past her into the kitchen. 'Why do you have to try to con me into believing a lot of hocus-pocus? I know none of it's true! Why can't you be honest with me?' She turned away. 'You know I have to stay if it's best for Mother. I'll do it to please her. She means so much to me. I can't bear to think of her——' her voice choked '—of her being made ill by all this.'

He didn't reply, and when she turned back his face was a wooden mask. Eventually he said, 'You know what marriage entails. I need your full agreement.'

'You're so hard, Marlow. You have no right to force me to—to *sleep* with you.' Flame blushed violently at the thoughts flooding through her head.

'Sleep is the last thing I'm interested in,' he said contemptuously. He went on, 'I want you, Flame. You're my wife. If I can't have you in my bed, who can I have?'

'I didn't realise *marriage* was a prerequisite,' she retorted.

He ignored that. 'Six months. She'll be out of danger by then. Is it long?'

'It's *forever*.' Flame shuddered, closing her eyes as the enormity of what she was conceding hit her. Could she cope with the aftermath of six months of living with a man like Marlow? It was bad enough being forced into an agreement, but her insatiable physical need for him was stronger than ever. How could she cope when he was no longer there?

Then she comforted herself with the perverse hope that it might turn out to be the best method of slaking herself of her crazy, mindless obsession for him, for surely, when she lived with him at close quarters, desire would exhaust itself, leaving her heart-free at last?

'You'll have to give me a day or so to get—to get used to the idea,' she faltered.

He nodded. 'We have plenty of time ahead of us.' He began to go through the cupboards and seemed to know exactly where everything was. It told her how firmly he had got himself wedged into the household. But he was, as Samantha had said, she recalled bitterly, one of the family.

'Salad,' he announced, emerging from the walk-in cool-room, 'and cheese, sardines, bread, olives——'

'Anything for me—I don't care. It'll all taste like sawdust.'

He looked at her over his shoulder with raised eyebrows as he placed everything on the table.

In order to quench the unbearable silence that hung over them she said, 'I can't quite understand why I wasn't told Mother was ill when it first happened.'

'I advised Sam not to tell you. I didn't want you——' Marlow seemed to hesitate.

'What?' she prompted, wondering what he was about to admit.

'I was going to say I didn't want you worried, but in view of what you said to me just now I wonder if you would regard that as another sign of hypocrisy?' He turned to look at her, his face bleak, the blue eyes empty.

Flame bit her lip. 'It would be, wouldn't it? I can't see you caring a damn whether I was worried or not.'

He shrugged, and his lips set in a hard line. 'Perhaps you're right,' he agreed with a sarcastic edge. 'Who knows?' He looked down at the things spread out on the kitchen table. 'If you want a villain, Flame, say so.' He turned and his eyes swept hers soullessly. 'I'll oblige you any time.'

'Of course you will,' she said, trying not to feel chilled by that look. 'You'll do anything to get your hands on what you want.'

He jerked round to face her. 'Is it my success that rankles with you? I learned the hard way to fight for what I want. Those who don't fight, don't want. Of course,' he gave a mirthless smile, 'what we believe worth fighting for can often turn out to be worthless once we've got it. But that's another matter.'

Still trying to fathom the enigma of this reply, she watched as he deftly split a flat loaf, spread it with butter and stacked it with salad and cheese. He repeated the exercise, then picked one of them up and walked rapidly towards the kitchen door with it.

'There's your lunch. Forgive me if I don't join you,' he said. He went out, closing the door quietly between them.

Half afraid he had been going to demand his conjugal rights straight away despite what she had said about needing a few days to get used to the idea, Flame felt deflated as soon as he left. Picking at what passed for lunch, she wondered why she hadn't told him more clearly that she knew the true reason why he wanted to prolong their marriage. She wondered how long it would take for the question of the will to be sorted out. Perhaps when it was all made watertight he would then think fit to release her from their diabolical alliance.

Wearing a strapless voile dress with a boned bodice, its shades of amber subtly toned to the colour of her hair, Flame said goodnight to her mother, then went outside. Emilio gave her an appreciative glance as she came out on to the terrace. 'So you've decided to come with us this evening?'

Samantha beamed at her. 'It'll do us all good to let our hair down a little. I haven't liked to leave Mother too often. It'll be nice to get out, won't it, darling?' She and Emilio were looped in each other's arms like newlyweds. Flame shivered at the thought. Fortunately, Marlow was nowhere to be seen.

'Is it far?' she asked, deliberately not mentioning his whereabouts as they went towards the car parked at the front.

'No, but we'll take the scenic route, then you can see the beginnings of Playa del Rey.' And to Flame's unspoken question Samantha went on, 'That's the name we chose for Marlow's new beach village. It's going to look absolutely wonderful when it's finished—all Andalusian arches and courtyards and fountains. I wouldn't mind living there myself!'

Emilio shepherded the two women into the car, making a great deal of fuss over Samantha as if her pregnancy was further on than it was, and then the white convertible was whispering down the drive to the main road.

All Flame could think was that it was a relief that Marlow had obviously decided not to come. She hadn't seen him since he'd stalked out of the kitchen, presumably to eat his lunch and then, she assumed, to go to his down-town office.

The development at Playa del Rey—Beach of the King, Flame translated with an ironic inward smile—was mainly just building site—heavy plant and mounds of raw orange earth, with here and there bright yellow plastic piping coiled like enormous sleeping snakes—but under Samantha's enthusiastic guidance she saw the possibilities. Most of the villas would be built on the steep sides of a ravine, leaving a jungle of palms intact further up to shelter the village from the main coast road. It would be secluded and, if Samantha was to be believed, very beautiful.

'We still own the land, Mother tells me,' remarked Flame as they made their way back over the dusty track to where the car was parked. 'But Marlow owns the buildings.'

'Yes, why?' Samantha frowned.

'Nothing,' replied Flame. 'I just wondered if you knew.'

'Naturally. Marlow has discussed everything with us. When the money starts coming in from the villa rentals and so forth, we two, as directors of Montrose Holdings and leasors of the land to one of Marlow's companies, will get a share of the profits. Because your attitude has been so uncertain with regard to Marlow, Mother wanted to make sure you wouldn't do anything stupid, like trying to block Marlow's freedom to develop the land the way he wants. Personally I'm more than willing to leave it to him as I'm convinced he knows best.' Samantha paused when Flame slowed down to have one final look at the site and Emilio, back first, honked the car horn to tell them to hurry up.

Flame didn't say anything else. No doubt the matter would be thoroughly discussed later, especially if the uncomfortable matter of the will was going to be brought up.

When they arrived at a large villa in one of the outlying districts of the town, Samantha and Emilio seemed to know everyone.

'I'll tell you who they all are as we go along,' whispered Samantha as they went out on to a terrace strung with lights. 'A lot of ex-pats, and business contacts, of course,' she pulled a face, 'but Rosa and Marcos are old friends of ours. Marcos is a lawyer specialising in property law and works for the consortium.'

Flame raised her eyebrows, but just then someone came up with a tray of drinks and they were plunged into a whirl of introductions. Feeling a little numbed by it all as her missing night's sleep began to catch up with her, Flame merely coasted from one group to the next, eventually finding herself standing beside the large pool with a tall, rather handsome Spaniard named Rafael. After he had introduced himself he told her he was Marcos's junior partner.

Together they admired the last streaks of the setting sun as it slid behind the foothills of the sierra. It was a romantic scene. Rafael went away to refill Flame's glass and when he returned to find a group of new arrivals surging over to join them he took her by the elbow.

'I hope you'll sit beside me at dinner,' he asked, his eyes luminous with something more than just that simple request.

'Actually,' blurted Flame, carefully disengaging her arm, 'I don't know whether you know I'm married.' She bit her lip at the thought, and when Rafael raised his eyebrows and asked, 'But where is this negligent husband of yours?' she blushed and was just about to shrug off her ignorance when a pair of dazzling blue eyes found and caught her own.

Her mouth sagged, then collecting her wits she managed to croak, 'Actually he's just arrived...' then her voice trailed away. Marlow had indeed arrived. But he was not alone.

Rafael turned and took in the situation at once. Marlow was accompanied by an attractive blonde, and it was obvious he was as surprised to see Flame as she was to see him.

She felt Rafael take her arm again in a casually friendly gesture. 'Perhaps you will still sit next to me at dinner?' he murmured in her ear.

But Flame's eyes were now firmly riveted on the woman standing beside Marlow. Her face was not unfamiliar.

Last time she had seen her she had worn all the hallmarks of outraged surprise. It wasn't surprising—she had been in Marlow's bed at the time.

Flame felt the blood slowly drain from her face. Her limbs became strangely heavy. Then to her mystification the scene before her seemed to ebb. She put out a hand to draw it back, and somewhere a glass fell to the marble tiles, shattering with an endless scatter of sound that caused a momentary lull in the conversation of those standing nearest. Then she felt a strong arm take hold of her round the waist. Someone said something in Spanish and then she felt the crowd open and close behind her as she was half carried, ebbing in and out of darkness, to a seat in a quiet corner of the terrace.

'It's all right,' came a harsh voice almost at once, 'I'll take over.'

A hand pushed her head down below her knees, then suddenly everything came flooding back in full colour and the sound was switched up, causing her to lift her head to find out who had taken charge. Marlow was scowling down at her. It was his hand on the back of her neck. She pushed it off, then smiled up at the still hovering Rafael.

'Meet my husband,' she said weakly, 'or have you already met? And yes,' she went on as her voice became stronger, 'I accept your invitation, Rafael, thank you.' She rose to her feet, disguising the fact that she still felt wobbly by shaking out her long flame-coloured hair where Marlow's handling had flattened it. There was an uncontrollable trembling in her knees and she stumbled before she could stop herself.

Marlow's hand came out to steady her at the same moment as Rafael's, and the two men glowered at one another. 'I said,' gritted Marlow, 'I'll take over. Would you get her a glass of water, perhaps, if you want to be helpful?'

Rafael's dark eyes smouldered, but with a glance at Flame's pale face and another hurried glance at the jut of Marlow's chin he moved towards the house.

'I thought he was never going to go,' gritted Marlow when he turned to Flame. 'What the hell's wrong? You're not pregnant, are you?'

'Don't be so ridiculous!' she spat. For a moment Marlow's eyes had burned like blue flame, only resuming the familiar soullessness at her spontaneous denial. She tossed her head. 'What do you think I am?'

'I can only imagine what you got up to in London. Running wild. That's why you went, isn't it? And this lover of yours may not be as careful as he could be——'

'How *dare* you?'

'What?' he broke in swiftly. 'Malign the devil in his absence? Bring him over. Let's have it out face to face—I'm ready.'

'Anybody would think you were jealous!' she hissed.

'Just playing the part to the hilt,' he murmured as Rafael returned. 'Don't forget I am your loving *husband*, darling.' He deliberately let Rafael overhear this last endearment and crowned it by pressing a husbandly kiss on the side of her face. With a silent glance Rafael handed Flame the glass of water, then melted back into the crowd. 'Wise man,' observed Marlow, with a smug smile.

'Maybe he'll keep your *friend* occupied?' she said sweetly.

'Friend?' Marlow must have known who she meant, but he quirked an eyebrow in feigned ignorance.

'*Mistress*, should I say?' Flame gripped the glass with such force she was surprised it didn't shatter between her fingers. But Marlow showed neither anger nor surprise at her accusation, and she could only marvel at his self-control. To look at that harsh, blank face you would have thought she hadn't said a thing!

She made herself force the tension from her body, but inside she was still reeling from the shock of seeing Marlow's mistress again. In her imagination the woman had grown into a nightmare figure, larger than life, an artful Jezebel, practising her seductive charms on a far too willing victim. But Flame had always pictured her as someone belonging to the past, not as current news and obviously still enjoying an intimate relationship with Marlow.

The shock made her feel choky. But there was no point in having a slanging match with Marlow in front of a crowd of strangers. Or anywhere, come to that. He obviously had his own life. A mere marriage of convenience such as theirs wasn't going to have any effect on his behaviour.

Marlow was leading her by the arm now and when she focused properly she saw he was making straight back to where his mistress was chatting vivaciously to a group of people by the pool. 'I want you to meet my wife,' he said to the group at large, but it was on the blonde that his glance rested. Warning her, thought Flame through a cloud of misery.

The woman held out a hand heavy with rings. 'Hi,' she said huskily, 'I'm Victoria, Marlow's dogsbody.'

Dazedly Flame stared at her. It seemed a strange way to refer to the services she no doubt still performed for Marlow. Her derision must have shown on her face, for the woman added, 'His personal assistant, that is.'

Very personal, thought Flame in silent jealousy. She felt Marlow move impatiently beside her. 'She fainted just now,' she heard him say. 'I think she's still a little dazed. It must have been the sleepless night she's just had.' He turned to her. 'I expected you to be catching up on your sleep this evening.'

'Obviously,' she managed to say. Victoria was still staring at her, one hand outstretched, but realising that Flame wasn't going to take it she shrugged and gave her a puzzled smile.

'That night flight from Gatwick? I know it well.' Her lustrous brown eyes exchanged a glance with Marlow. Then she turned back to Flame. 'I'm sure we haven't met, but your face seems somehow familiar——'

'No! That's right, we haven't. I've—I've been living in London for some time,' agreed Flame in confusion. She was too shaken to face all the ramifications of blurting out the truth right now.

'Pursuing an independent career,' appended Marlow in a mocking tone.' He noticed then that Victoria's glass was nearly empty and, taking it familiarly from her fingers, went off in pursuit of a refill, leaving the two women together. How confident he must be feeling, thought Flame watching him go. She turned to Victoria.

'How long have you—have you worked for him?' she managed to get out. Some desperation goaded her to discover what she could, but Victoria's answer plunged her into deeper despair.

'Oh, we go back a long way, Marlow and I,' she replied airily. 'Over six years. But,' she went on, 'I was based with his subsidiary on Ibiza most of that time. It wasn't until a few months ago that Marlow insisted I move over here and work directly from his main office. I liked the island,' she went on chattily, 'but after so long I felt I'd had enough. I feel much closer to the action over here.'

'Six years is a long time,' offered Flame weakly. She tortured herself with the supposition that Victoria had been Marlow's mistress all that time—all the time he was courting her, telling her all those lies about loving her. But how had he talked away his wedding day? Or had Victoria been so far from the action, as she had put it, that she hadn't known about it? Had he deceived them both for a time?

'If you've been around all that time,' said Flame, conscious that the remark sounded vaguely catty, 'you must have been at our wedding. It was eighteen months ago.'

'Yes,' Victoria frowned. 'I remember organising the flowers. It was a special order from a horticulturist near San Antonio. But I couldn't make the actual reception.' She offered no explanation, but Flame saw at once that Marlow had managed things very well. How he'd got his mistress to organise flowers for his marriage to someone else made her mind boggle. Unless, she thought, there had been a pretty powerful incentive of some sort.

She wondered what it might be. Love, lust or money, she judged. But did it matter?

Just then Marlow returned with Victoria's refill. He gave a cursory glance at the glass of water Flame still clutched between her fingers. 'Maybe you'd better stay with that,' he suggested. 'I'll run you home in a few minutes.'

'Don't bother.' She drew herself up. 'I'm fine. I wouldn't dream of upsetting your evening.' Bristling at the idea that he was trying to get her out of the way, Flame swept across the terrace, blindly walking past the chattering groups that were just beginning to go in to supper until Samantha and Emilio caught up with her and guided her towards the open sliding doors leading into the dining-room.

'Lovely party, isn't it?' exclaimed her sister at once. 'Come and sit next to us.' Obviously she hadn't observed Flame's faint, but as they moved into the dining-room Rafael appeared beside her.

'Feeling better?' he asked, bending his dark head when he saw she was minus Marlow.

'Much, thank you.'

'Are you unwell?'

Flame shook her head. 'Tired. And,' she couldn't help adding, 'a little bit surprised to meet my husband too.' Marlow had treated Rafael abominably—after all, he had only been trying to help. Now he took her arm.

'So I get my wish after all?' He had already taken in the fact that Marlow was lingering on the terrace with the same woman with whom he had arrived. It occurred to Flame then that he probably knew about their affair and was trying to make it clear to her that he knew without actually saying so. It was a small community; probably everyone knew about it. The thought made her tingle with humiliation. It would account for everyone's kindness this evening. She wondered if it also explained Samantha's sudden start of guilt when she had asked her that question earlier about Marlow's girlfriends. She resolved to have it out with her later.

Senses tuned to pick up any undercurrent in the conversations around her, Flame allowed herself to be escorted in to supper. She hadn't imagined any misery to match the depths into which she was now plunged.

CHAPTER FIVE

RAFAEL was an attentive and charming escort, but Flame couldn't help but be aware of one or two odd looks being cast in their direction. Puzzling a little, she found the explanation not long in coming. Samantha took her to one side when the meal was over and, under a pretence of showing her where the bathroom was, pushed her inside and closed the door.

'What *do* you think you're doing?' she demanded when they were alone.

Flame looked at her in bewilderment.

'You really don't know, do you?' Samantha knew her younger sister well enough to realise that the look of innocent bewilderment on her face was genuine. 'Don't you realise you're on *trial*, Flame? People know you walked out on Marlow straight after the wedding. Now all they can see is that you've suddenly come back—and straight away you're chatting up another man! The Spanish take that sort of thing seriously. It's seen as a blatant act of infidelity. Marlow must feel about two inches high.'

'Oh, don't be ridiculous, Sam! *Infidelity?* If you mean with Rafael, I'm only chatting to him as if we were two ordinary human beings. What on earth's wrong with that?'

'Everything. The main thing being that you should be by your husband's side.'

'But he's already got somebody by his side. Or hadn't you noticed?'

'You mean Victoria?'

'Of course I mean Victoria!'

'You're still his wife, Flame. Not that marriage appears to mean much to you.' Samantha's expression was severe. 'Marlow happens to have brought along his personal assistant. It's not unusual. He has to talk business. Marcos's invitations always include the opportunity to make new contacts. You just have to go along with it.'

'Victoria is hardly a new contact,' argued Flame bitterly.

'No, but the group they've been introduced to are. No doubt that's why Marlow brought her along—to meet them.'

'No doubt!' Flame's sarcasm made Samantha frown.

'It's your duty to shelve your differences in public,' she told her. 'This is a small community. You can do immense harm to Marlow's personal reputation if you're seen to be unreliable. Actually, I'm surprised at Rafael. He should know better.'

'Perhaps he doesn't go along with your antiquated views, Sam. I must say I'm flabbergasted to hear you of all people coming out with things like this.' The two sisters glared at each other in the bright strip-light of the luxurious bathroom in which they were standing, then at the same moment they both relented.

'I'm sorry, love——' Samantha took Flame by the arms.

'I didn't realise it mattered a damn what I did,' mumbled Flame.

'I had to warn you. And it's not fair on Rafael either.'

'You mean I'm giving him the wrong impression?' Flame's eyes widened a fraction.

Samantha nodded. 'He knows, as does everybody, that you've both been living apart. The way you've behaved tonight will only have convinced him that your return isn't meant to be a serious reconciliation——'

'Nor is it!' cut in Flame with a clenching of her hands.

Samantha gave her a studying look. 'You know what I think about you and Marlow? I don't believe you really know what you're doing——'

'Why can't you and Mother stand by me? Why do you have to be on *his* side all the time?' Flame burst out.

'It's not like that, Flame. We are on your side and we both know how head over heels in love you were—both of you. It was a real love match,' Samantha countered gently.

'Sure it was. And he was so cut up when I walked out, wasn't he?'

'Yes, as it happens. More than you probably realise——'

'Don't give me that!' Flame gave a disbelieving scowl.

'He was like a man in a nightmare,' Samantha went on remorselessly. 'Then he seemed to make the decision to throw himself into his work. To begin with it was like a sort of frenzy, as if he was trying to block out the pain.' She frowned. 'He'd hate me for telling you this.'

'I don't believe it anyway,' Flame came back bitterly. 'I obviously know more about Marlow than you. I've seen behind the scenes, thank you.'

'He didn't——' Samantha bit her lip. 'He didn't beat you, did he?'

'*What?* I should hope not!'

'Then I can't understand why you feel so bitter about him.'

'He married me to get his hands on the land—you must have guessed that! I only realised when I discovered he could deceive on other levels too.' Flame averted her head. 'You're trying to tell me he cared a damn when I left? If he had,' she turned back with a smile of bitter triumph, 'he would have come after me, wouldn't he?'

Samantha slowly shook her head. 'I don't think so. He can be as stiff-necked as you when he wants. The last thing he would do would be to chase after somebody who'd rejected him. That's his childhood coming out, I suppose.'

'His *what*?' Flame gave her sister a sharp glance.

'His stepfather not wanting him around and all that. He must have told you?'

Flame shook her head, pretending she didn't want to hear, but impatient for Samantha to go on nevertheless.

'He still feels bitter about not being reconciled with his mother before she died. His stepfather had made it plain he didn't want a seventeen-year-old boy around when he married his mother. That's when Marlow ran away to sea.'

'I didn't know he'd done that,' Flame retorted somewhat stiffly.

'Maybe there are other things you don't know.'

'I know enough, thank you!'

'Do you know how good to us he's been?'

'There's a lot in it for him.'

'Don't be cynical,' said Samantha.

'You don't imagine he'd put himself out for the Montrose Clan, as he calls us, for nothing, do you?'

'Maybe we're the family he's never had.'

Flame felt tears like red-hot needles behind her eyes. 'Damn him to hell!' She turned and groped for the handle of the bathroom door.

'Wait, Flame! If you really don't want to attempt a reconciliation, you'll just have to say so. But if that's your decision I think you should be very careful how you tell Mother. She's still very weak.' Samantha sighed and bit her lip. 'I feel torn three ways. I want you to be happy, and Mother—and Marlow as well.'

'And my actions are the key to it all.' Flame bent her head. The floor on which she stood was done in a marble checkerboard pattern. At that moment she felt like one of the pieces in a game. She only had to wait and someone would reach down and place her in another square. She longed to break out of the game, but how could she? Samantha had summed it up clearly enough. It wasn't just her own happiness that was at stake. It was also possibly her mother's life, if the hints she had received from all sides were to be understood correctly.

'I've already told Marlow I agree to a retrial,' she spoke with bitter irony, 'I'll——' she licked her lips, a little nervous at what lay ahead '—I'll go back, give Rafael the cold shoulder, then sit at Marlow's feet for the rest of the evening. Will that be sufficient?' She tried to smile.

'No need to go to extremes. I'll talk to Rafael if you like. We're good friends. In fact, I'd jolly well like to know what he thinks he's up to—compromising my sister in public like this!'

They exchanged smiles, Samantha with a hint of warning in her blue eyes, Flame with a resignation that momentarily masked the deep misery she felt.

Together they went back to join the party.

When Flame found Marlow he was leaving one group and had just greeted some new arrivals. He turned as she approached and his friends went on into the house to find their host and hostess. Victoria was nowwhere in sight and they were suddenly alone.

'You should have warned me you were going to be here and it was going to be an exercise in public relations this evening. I thought it was just a friendly get-together,' Flame began somewhat defensively.

Marlow raised his eyebrows. 'Why, what difference would it have made?'

She shrugged and dropped her glance. 'I'd have played the role of supportive wife to better effect,' she mumbled.

'Don't worry. Not everyone knows we're supposed to be together.' Despite his words there was an ill-concealed hostility in the finely honed features. It was a shock to discover how massively attractive he looked in formal evening clothes, ambiguously charming in his dinner-jacket, like some jungle animal for the moment pretending to be tame. But the raw masculinity of the predator beneath was blatantly evident.

Under the pretence of reaching for one of her hands he gripped her wrist tightly between finger and thumb, holding it by his side, forcing her to skirt the edge of the pool with him to where a low wall at the far end of the terrace dropped sheer to the main road. Like a prisoner she was marched to a secluded spot further along in the shelter of some trees, and there he swung her round to face him with such force that their bodies met in an unexpected collision. She was made sickeningly aware of his physical power. For a second it made her senses swim, sexual desire flaring uncontrollably, before she recovered sufficiently to step back.

He released her wrist at once, eyes narrowing as he registered the effect of the accidental contact of their bodies, then he gave a derisive chuckle.

'Control yourself, Flame. Or is it the prospect of Rafael's lovemaking that makes you so responsive?'

She felt her hands clench and would have given anything to slap the scathing look from off his face. Instead she turned to look at the view as if that had been the purpose of their escape.

But Marlow had only just started. Moving close behind her, he placed both hands on the wall on either side of her hips and pressed his body suggestively against hers. His mouth quested over the back of her neck beneath the long fall of hair and she was trapped while he forced her to endure the tantalising pressure over her exposed skin. The heat of open sexual desire poured off him, enveloping her in helpless waves of expectation, summoning visions of pleasure she feared to admit.

Holding herself rigid beneath the increasingly intimate movements of his body against her own, she tried to bring a protest to her lips, but his hands were already sliding over her breasts in the strapless sun-dress, expertly unfastening the three buttons that held it in place, hot fingers sliding at once into the opening, searching out the honeyed softness of her breasts, his thumb caressing the give-away hardness of her nipples with movements that brought a feeling of helpless abandon to her love-starved senses.

He showed no sign of recognising any boundaries, and after an initial protest she found herself being carried helplessly along on the crest of his desire. Would it be wrong to give in? drummed the question in her head as his body told her of his need. Would it? *Would it...?* she thought as her own body succumbed to its natural urge. She wanted him so much, no matter what she had tried to tell herself over the last nightmare months. 'Marlow...?' she breathed, half questing for words to match her feelings, hoping in the wildness of her hunger to hear words from his lips to mirror those she dared not speak aloud.

But instead she only heard him mutter feverishly against the side of her head with words expressing physical desire, words of a primitive, male, merely sexual hunger.

Then his tongue searched the secret caverns of her mouth, traced a sliding trail down the side of her neck, discovered the route to greater pleasure, coming down the path between her breasts, moistening her nipples, taking her breasts one by one in his mouth as he turned her into his arms, lifting her against him, her body moulded against his own, her own helpless moans mingling with the stertorous sound of his breathing.

'I can always count on this—your weakness, Flame. Your hopeless weakness.' She felt him lift his head and his voice lashed softly, asking, 'Are you like this with everyone?'

Aware that his body was still pulsing against her own with no attempt to conceal his desire, she opened her eyes, shivering when she saw the savage expression on his face, his eyes blue ice-chips, piercing hers as if to winkle the truth from her. With an obvious effort he held himself in check, control checked only with difficulty as she could see. If her own control had not been swamped so completely a feeling of anger at the overt denigration of her morals would have made her fight back, but her longing to experience the climax to the wild frenzy into which he had so rapidly whipped her weakened her anger, and instead she felt tears sting along her eyes because such ecstasy of the senses so plainly lacked the deeper feelings of love.

Miserably she tried to calm her unsatisfied longing, leaning against him for a moment as she tried to restore herself, trying not to respond to the involuntary movements that still betrayed his desire, though she longed for him to take her in his arms and love her totally.

'It's no good if we don't love each other,' she muttered in a fever of despair. 'I thought—I hoped——'

'Lack of feeling can't be helped. Don't blame yourself for this. I'll take the blame. All of it.' He spoke savagely, admitting to her surprise, 'We suffer the same weakness—we're alike in that—wanting and loving aren't the same. At least——' He broke off as if unwilling to go on. Then suddenly his anger heightened. 'This is useless! What the hell are you turning me into?' His eyes glinted and he began to fasten up her bodice with rough fingers, smoothing back her hair ungently until only the flush in her cheeks and the swollen scarlet of her lips told the tale of the last few minutes.

His stern, rather hawklike profile was chiselled against the night sky as he turned. 'I didn't drag you down here for this.' His voice grated. 'Hell, we've got a bed to go to—a marriage bed, no less. We don't have to behave like a couple of teenagers on a date.' He gave a bitter smile as if to disown the self-disgust that seemed to be shaking through him. 'I guess you kind of took me by surprise, Flame. I hope it makes you feel good to know how much power you've got over my baser animal instincts.' His lips twisted. 'You'd better tell Rafael I nearly broke his neck back there. Warn him. I'm a jealous man where my possessions are concerned. I won't be responsible if he tries that on again.'

Still no mention of the word she longed to hear on his lips. It was obviously reserved for Victoria. 'There's no need to be melodramatic!' she retorted. 'I didn't realise I was doing anything that could be misunderstood,' she told him, her voice shaky, the rhythm of her aroused blood beating in ever-receding waves that took her further from the demi-paradise she had yearned to enter.

Feeling hugely cheated, yet relieved too that the situation, becoming totally and rapidly out of hand, had not developed further, she moved out of range, becoming aware of the distant sound of partying still emanating from the terrace. In the shadows at the bottom of the garden they were out of sight of other guests. She smoothed her dress again with shaking hands.

'Hadn't we better go back?' she suggested. 'Victoria will be wondering where you are, won't she?' Unhappiness made her voice acerbic.

'She's left,' Marlow told her shortly.

'Of course.' Her former coldness returned completely. 'Obviously you wouldn't be here with me like this if she were still around.'

'Probably not.' He smiled faintly. 'But I could always plead that I was led astray. It was you who sought me out, I seem to remember. Remorse, was it? Or did somebody say something that pricked your conscience?'

'Go to hell, Marlow!' Flame was furious with herself now that she was coming to her senses. Furious for falling for him. For allowing him to see how much she desired him.

At least she hadn't uttered the words that had begged to be spoken—the unconscious words dredged from deep within her soul, humiliating words that would have told of her love too. But maybe it wasn't love after all. Perhaps she was simply too inexperienced to tell the difference between this wild obsession for his touch and the steady, long-lasting deeper emotion of love. Violently she wished it were so. Between love and desire, surely desire would fade the sooner?

Her eyes drank in the harsh profile, the familiar slant of his pronounced cheekbones, the tempting hollows when he drew his lips back in one of those remembered smiles, and she longed to see beneath the superficial accident of skin and bone that made him so desirable to her, to see beneath it, to the *truth* of what he really felt and thought and wanted. He turned, abrupt, harsh, his eyes two indigo slits, assessing her silence.

Well, she wouldn't allow it to be love, she told herself. And she wouldn't allow him to think it might be.

She lifted the cold oval of her face to his in the darkness. 'You're quite a stud, Marlow. I'd forgotten that,' she lied. 'I'm not surprised Victoria is such a perennial. Why should marriage make her let you go? She must be quite smitten. I suppose that's what you were counting on to keep her sweet when you made your move to marry me? Plus your fabulous wealth, of course, about which no one can be in doubt.'

His head jerked. 'What the hell's our marriage got to do with Victoria?'

'Nothing, apparently!' Flame turned and began to walk rapidly up the garden. He was slow to follow her. She was already walking up the steps to the terrace when she heard him behind her.

'Time to go home?' His voice cracked like a whip.

'I'll go back with Sam and Emilio.'

'You won't. You'll leave with me.'

She gave a dismissive laugh, but when she reached the terrace he was still by her side and Emilio and Samantha had already left. Rosa seemed surprised she should be asking for them. Naturally she would expect Flame to leave with her husband.

As it was, they looked like any other married couple as they said their farewells side by side and went out to the forecourt where Marlow's car was parked.

'Stay at the main house as long as you like, Flame. It would obviously be for the best,' he said as soon as he cut the engine when they reached Santa Margarita.

'What about Mother——?' she began.

'For heaven's sake. I'm not going to bed you to please your mother!'

'I mean, she'll guess we haven't patched things up——'

'So stay in the *casita* if it keeps everyone happy. There's a spare room. Give me a day or two to get it fixed. I'm not sure I want what you've turned into.' He leaned across to open the passenger door, noting with a hardening of his expression the way she flinched as his arm grazed her breasts, but he didn't say anything beyond a curt goodnight.

Flame swayed on the gravel for a moment, then heard him close the car door. He stayed in the car, sitting inside in the darkness. She wondered if he was waiting to watch her go into the house safely—a longing for some sign of feeling other than mere lust raising expectations—but as soon as she inserted her key in the lock, the engine purred to life again. She saw the car slide off down the lane, back the way they had just come, back, she surmised, towards the town. It wasn't difficult to guess that his destination would be the apartment of his mistress.

Tears of anger and frustration and something she knew was deep sorrow filled her eyes. But she was so tired now that when she finally undressed and climbed into bed, as soon as her head touched the pillow, sleep claimed her.

CHAPTER SIX

WHEN Flame woke up next morning she lay cocooned in the warmth of a light duvet for a few minutes, a band of sunlight across her face. It was this that had woken her. For a moment she couldn't remember where she was, then memory flooded back. It was Spanish sunlight pushing its way through the slats of the carelessly closed blinds, not the watery March sunlight of England. She sat up. Something about the deep stillness of the morning told her it was late. She slid out of bed and opened the blinds with a smack. On the terrace was evidence that the children had been having elevenses, but there was no sign of anyone. The pool lay like a splinter of lapis lazuli, glinting in the sun.

She turned back and scrabbled in her travel bag for her tiny clock, then blinked. It was half-past eleven already. She wondered what time Marlow had returned. Or if he had returned at all.

Maybe he had gone straight to the down-town office after breakfasting with Victoria. She tried to push the thought away.

After hanging up her things—not that she'd bothered to bring much, having been under the impression that her visit was only going to be a short one—she showered and put on a pair of shorts and a T-shirt. Hair still damp, she then made her way to her mother's room. But when she poked her head round the door the nurse silently shook her head. Sybilla was still asleep, her face slightly flushed, though whether this was a good or bad sign Flame couldn't tell. 'Would you like a cup of coffee?' she mouthed to the nurse. The nurse nodded, but got to her feet and came out into the corridor.

'I'll come down with you.'

Flame found her way around the once-familiar kitchen with a shock of recognition, like someone slipping on an old pair of slippers. It was good to be here because despite everything it was still home. 'Is there anything I can do to make myself useful?' she asked.

The nurse shook her head. 'There's so little to do. Your mother has a very well run household—Mr Hudson makes sure of that.'

Flame smiled faintly. Good for Mr Hudson! Even the temporary staff were apparently eating out of his hand.

'Where is everyone this morning?' she asked, refusing to let her mind dwell on unpleasantness on such a lovely morning.

'*La señora* is at the beach with the children.'

'Calahonda?' Flame referred to the public beach ten minutes' walk round the headland. But the nurse shook her head.

'At Santa Margarita.' This was the private cove at the bottom of the cliff path. It was reached by hundreds of tiny steps set in the cliff face, and Flame was surprised that Samantha had dragged all the way down there with the children when there was the far less difficult though longer walk to the nearby public beach.

'I'll join them later.' She pressed the plunger on the *cafetière* and poured the steaming liquid into two wide cups. The nurse stayed chatting for a few minutes, then returned to her duties.

Flame realised again that she was at a loose end. There seemed nothing useful for her to do and she hadn't come round to the idea of simply being on holiday. Only two days ago she had been in the middle of organising an exhibition for a group of computer companies, run off her feet and relishing the challenge. Now she was idle, with no proper role. No wonder she felt restless, she told herself.

What would be the wifely duties expected of her, bar the obvious? she wondered grimly. Did Marlow expect her to busy herself with domestic matters? From what the nurse had said and judging by what she had seen herself they would amount to very little. She wouldn't even be allowed to do any cooking. After acquiring a suntan, what then?

Thinking about work made her think of Johnny. She really ought to ring him and let him know she wouldn't be coming back. He wouldn't be best pleased. In fact he had every right to be livid. She hoped and prayed the new temp was as good as the agency claimed.

She poured herself another cup of coffee, staving off the moment when she knew she would have to pick up the phone. It was just as she was telling herself that she couldn't delay any longer that the kitchen door opened and she sensed Marlow come in.

He walked noiselessly across the tiled floor, and only when she felt him standing over her did she raise her head. How had she known it was him? she wondered with a shiver as she met his glance. It was the old telepathy, as alive as ever, despite everything else that lay between them.

He was looking more handsome than he should in an old pair of white trousers and a plain white shirt that could have done with an iron. On his feet was a pair of scruffy-looking espadrilles that she was sure he had been wearing eighteen months ago. His dark hair was tousled as if his hands had been raked through it many times, and his expression became severe when their eyes met.

'I hope you're thoroughly rested,' he growled, sounding as if she were committing some felony merely by sitting in the kitchen at mid-morning. 'I could do with a cup of coffee if you've time.' His blue eyes challenged hers as if expecting some bitter riposte, and when she rose to her feet she felt a twinge of satisfaction to note the surprise in them.

So that he didn't imagine she was being merely compliant she said, 'I was wondering how I could make myself useful. I'll make a fresh pot.'

Marlow was silent while she put the kettle back on and got out another cup and saucer, but when she leaned against the counter to wait for the water to boil he said, 'What are you doing the rest of the day?'

She shrugged. 'What do the wives of wealthy men do? Sunbathe, I suppose.'

'That's not *all* they do.' He didn't go on, but she knew instantly what was in his mind. She flushed, and flushed even more when he added, 'Luckily Rafael's work schedule is almost as heavy as mine and when *he's* free *I'm* free. I think even you might find the logistics of an affair with a man like that too intricate to handle.'

'I'm not looking for extra-marital affairs, Marlow.' Her tone was coated with ice. 'Besides,' she added sweetly, 'I only met him for the first time last night. I like to know a man properly before I——' She bit her lip, her nerve failing her as she caught his glance.

'You do, do you?' His eyes gave ice for ice. 'Well, don't count on getting to know *him* any better, will you?' His movements became savage as he abruptly crossed to the window, then he turned and flung himself into a wooden chair at the table, with a fierce, 'What the hell's wrong with that kettle?'

They both looked at it. 'It seems perfectly all right to me,' murmured Flame, wondering just why he was pretending to be so jealous when they both knew his reasons for wanting the marriage to go on had nothing to do with feelings and simply everything to do with money.

'You did a lot of running around in London, did you?' His eyes were storm-blue. 'Somehow I never thought you were the casual type.'

'You thought I was the stay-at-home type, I suppose. Willing to put up with anything.' She gave a bitter laugh. What he was suggesting was almost true—she had dated one or two men in London before Johnny, but they had always been kept at arm's length. Her feelings had been buried under a solid layer of permafrost. What Marlow had managed to make her feel again had shocked her with its violence, and she was still numbed by the volcanic disturbance to her equilibrium.

He was unwilling to leave the subject alone, however. 'I suppose you had plenty of opportunity working for— what was it?' He gave a bad impression of a man acting puzzled, and she almost smiled. 'Public relations? Is that what you called it?'

'You know full well it is. I did a course as soon as I reached London. You surely didn't expect me to do nothing, did you?' Flame frowned, remembering what he had told her earlier. 'I didn't guess that allowance was from you. I thought it came from Mother. I wouldn't have touched a penny of it if I'd known.'

'That's what I suspected,' he said drily. 'You'd have been happy running around London in rags, I suppose. I'm crazy, I suppose, to care whether my wife can make ends meet.'

He was being sarcastic, but she rose to the bait. 'What you mean is you just loved the idea of still being in control!'

Marlow gave a mocking laugh. 'If you say so. But I'd have stopped it pretty damn quick if I'd known you were sleeping around.'

'I did not sleep around!' she burst out, then turned, abruptly, angry with herself for being so transparent.

He gave a disbelieving smile. 'If you say so, darling.'

'You don't believe me, do you?'

'I don't see why I should believe one single word you say—even if you do shout,' he came back easily.

Her voice had hardly risen. 'I am not shouting,' she argued, deliberately softening her voice even more. 'Poor Marlow,' she went on sweetly, 'it must be hellish to suspect everybody else is as devious and double-dealing as you are yourself. You must feel you can't trust anybody.'

His lips twisted. 'I hope I'm nobody's fool,' he clipped. 'I trust when and where I've proof I can trust.

If I've been let down at all,' he went on unexpectedly, 'that's just life, isn't it?' His smile was more cynical than ever. 'Nobody's going to have me in tears just because they prove they're only human . . . I've come a long way since the days when I thought the world was painted either black or white.'

'There must be a lot of grey areas in your life!' Flame said smugly.

He gave her a sudden piercing glance. 'You never actually told me you wanted a career, Flame. Why didn't you say so? We could have discussed it properly.'

She looked away. A career had actually been something she hadn't thought about from the minute she set eyes on Marlow. It was crazy, the things a nineteen-year-old girl could feel, she thought now, snapping the lid off the coffee container. So far gone in the enchantment Marlow had seemed to weave, she had been willing to give up everything for him. 'Maybe it's all been for the best,' she said out loud. 'You would have turned me into a *Hausfrau* with nothing more important on my mind than how to arrange the flowers.'

'Don't you believe it,' he rasped. 'You know me better than that. I don't like helpless women.'

'No,' she stabbed, 'I suppose that's true. You prefer hard-boiled career women, don't you?'

'I do? How in hell do you know that, Flame?' His voice glowered suggestively. 'I suppose you know what else I like?'

'Sex,' she replied crisply. 'Plenty of it. So what? What's new? Aren't all men the same?'

'You tell me.' His voice held a note of quiet menace.

Flame bent her head, allowing a trail of amber hair to obscure her features. Why was he provoking her like this? Was he testing her? He must know she was as in-experienced now as when she had run out on him. Everything she knew she had been taught by him.

Careful with the cup she had accidentally over-filled, she placed it before him without looking at him. She could feel his eyes on her. But as she turned and made some sort of pretence at clearing up the mess on the work-top, she heard him give a sardonic laugh.

'What's all this? Am I supposed to be impressed? I certainly hadn't seen you as the domestic type.'

'What did you see me as, Marlow?' She turned, sud-denly angered by the cynical overtone of everything he had so far said. 'Don't answer that,' she bit out before he could reply. 'You saw me as a push-over—right? A stupid, naïve little child who couldn't tell when she was being made use of. You thought if you sweet-talked me into marriage you could get your hands on what you wanted. You thought I would never know. And you're right. I'm ashamed to admit it, but you were right. If I hadn't discovered you were capable of deceiving me——' She bit her lip. 'It was then, when I discovered what you were really like as a person, that I guessed your real reason for marrying me.'

'Real reason?' Marlow lifted his dark head.

But she didn't hear him. Her heart felt swollen as if full of a poison threatening to swamp her. She hated him. She loved him. And she wanted to be free of him to love a man she could respect, a man she could trust and care for, a man who would want her to bear his children and who would respect her and look after her in the way a husband was supposed to.

But Marlow and her own wayward heart had snatched all that away. She raised bitter green eyes to his. 'Why me, Marlow? Oh,' she gave a narrow laugh, 'don't answer that! Why not me? I was the one with the key to Cabo Santa Margarita, the richest jewel in your empire!'

He rose to his feet, the chair scraping harshly on the tiles, rage and desire vying in his face as he snatched up her slim body, dragging it hard against his own. 'You must have had thoughts like this before you married me,' he ground out. 'What corruption of the soul made you say you'd do it? What did you hope to get out of it?'

The hand that had clamped itself to her shoulder tightened and she tried to squirm away, but his body followed hers, forcing her back against the side of the kitchen table so that she could feel the hard edge of it grinding into the back of her thighs.

'Well?' he demanded ruthlessly. 'Are you going to answer me?'

Flame shook her head vigorously. 'I don't have to answer you. I don't have to do a thing you say. But I will answer this time.' She dropped her glance. 'I couldn't believe it. It had never entered my head that anybody would marry me to get their hands on Montrose property. It was totally outside my experience. It wasn't exactly as if I was an heiress, I'd hardly allowed Cabo Santa Margarita into my thoughts. It was simply a place where we lived, a lovely place built by Father for the family. It was simply my family home. I couldn't imagine anybody would need it, not until Mother suggested the idea.'

'I remember when she put it to me. I thought it was going to be a white elephant. I had more than enough land on my books. But she was very persuasive.' Marlow gave a bitter laugh. 'Then you appeared, like a princess in a fairy-tale. The Princess of Santa Margarita, no less.' He gazed long and silently into her face. 'Why did you do it? You still haven't told me. Why marry me?'

Her anger rose up, bringing emerald sparks to her eyes, and her voice was hoarse as she whispered, 'Did I have a *choice*?' And when he didn't reply straight away she said, 'You yourself decided you were going to marry me, come what may, and everybody else aided and abetted you. You deliberately set out to get me. It was nothing less than emotional rape.'

With a reluctance like the rallentando at the end of a symphony she felt his grip slacken finger by finger. She felt the heat of his body against hers begin to cool, to release her. Eventually he moved away, severing the contact.

His voice was strangely flat when he spoke. 'Many times I've thought it was a mistake, to meet you, marry you, all in the space of a few weeks. You were young then—young for your age, too, maybe. But I was impatient. I'm an impatient man, Flame, always have been. I'd done my living, knew what I wanted. And yes, there you were, the jewel in the crown.'

It wasn't quite what she had meant. It was Santa Margarita she saw as the jewel Marlow lusted for, but she let it pass as he want on, 'They do say, don't they, marry in haste, repent at leisure? I've had enough leisure, so-called, in the last eighteen months to repent a million times. I guess that goes for you too.' Then, surprisingly, he said, 'Forgive me, Flame. I shouldn't have done it…'

His face wore a look she had never seen before—vulnerable, uncertain, full of regrets. But before she could ponder over the unexpectedness of this it had changed again. He became his familiar brisk self, the man in control. 'I'm not going to let you go just yet. Call me a fool. Say I'm blind. But I can't let you go——' His eyes were full of horizons like the ocean they resembled. 'Maybe I don't know when I'm beaten, but I don't give in easily. And somehow I can't let things go just yet. I can't let *you* go. Hell, why should I?' She saw what she thought was pride etch his features, hardening them. 'You promised me six months and I'm going to keep you to it. But I give you my word, if you want to go after that I won't make things difficult.'

Flame held her breath, unsure whether this new act— Marlow looking unsure of himself, for goodness' sake!— was merely some new ploy, another trap into which she would walk in all innocence, for she didn't doubt he could make things very difficult should he choose. But then she looked at his expression and with a small shrug she gave her assent.

'There's no need for this. We've already agreed I'll stay and keep the façade intact, for Mother's sake,' she mumbled, shaken by the suspicion that she was not reading him properly. He seemed so unlike the autocratic savage she knew from the past. There were layers of uncertainty beneath the surface authority that were wholly new.

'I'll try not to pressure you,' he said. 'But we must have basic ground rules, don't you agree?'

Flame raised her head.

'Like respecting each other's dignity,' he went on.

Her eyes widened.

'I mean, of course, as far as other liaisons are concerned. Discretion, Flame. Give me that at least.'

He went on before she could bring any retort to her lips, angry or otherwise. 'I promise you the same.' His blue eyes probed, without guile. 'I'll keep you and care for you as my wife,' he continued. 'Be by my side when I need you. Give me loyalty. If it helps, remember that my empire, as you call it, belongs to us all. What's good for it is good for the family.'

'Except that you own the buildings and that's where the income comes from,' she bit out before Samantha's words came back to her. 'Oh, honestly!' she smoothed her hair impatiently. 'Do you *really* care about the family when it comes down to it?' Despite her air of certainty she searched his face for something, but it was carefully blank. 'Sam assures me that she and Emilio understand what's happening as far as the development is concerned,' she went on hurriedly. 'I hope it's true. I don't want you to go making fools of them as well.'

She rose to her feet, exhausted by the depth of emotion he had wished on her. They were like deep-sea divers and she was lost under the weight of the oceans, groping in the dark in a world she didn't understand.

'Marcos is as much Emilio's friend as mine. I trust him to work out some equitable arrangement should I want to break away from the Montrose name completely,' Marlow told her acidly.

'Hardly likely,' she muttered, thinking of the land he would lose.

He raised his eyes and for a moment she almost imagined she saw pain in their oceanic depths.

'Quite so,' he intoned through lips that scarcely moved.

She gave an impatient shake of her head. 'I think I'll go down to the beach. Samantha's down there with the children. She's probably expecting me.'

'I'll come with you. I'm feeling pretty bushed, actually.' His face was pale now she gave it a close look.

'Not enough sleep,' she clipped.

He gave a tired smile. 'I dare say you're right. It's going to be ten times worse when you move in.' His eyes glinted. 'Don't you want to come across to the *casita* and see your room?'

'I'll give it a miss right now,' she retorted. 'It'll no doubt still be there when I get back from the beach.'

Marlow rose and moved to the door when she did. 'You're not thinking of sunbathing dressed like that, are you? Where's the bikini?'

'If you're coming down——' Flame bit her lip. Her limbs trembled when he came close, but she strove to conceal the fact. He had played on her self-control enough this morning without forcing a repeat of last night's humiliating scene. Next time he touched her she would discover she had recovered from her weakness, as he called it. Strength would be her defence. But she wasn't going to give him any excuse for getting that close again.

She went out, saying over her shoulder, 'I'm probably as tanned as I'll get anyway. I don't tan much, as you may remember.' And then she was walking briskly across the terrace and through the garden, hoping he wouldn't attempt to keep up with her, and when he did so, ignoring him, jogging down the narrow cliff steps without giving him a chance to say anything more provoking than, 'Steady, you'll break your neck!'

She increased her pace, annoyed that he could keep up with her so easily, but pleased when Samantha and Britt waved them over straight away.

The children were playing happily by the water's edge and the two women had made themselves comfortable on the permanent loungers kept at the beach hut. Flame joined them, trying to ignore the fact that Marlow had stripped down to a pair of brief black swimming-trunks and thrown himself down beside her.

At first conversation ebbed and flowed in the sticky heat. Flame felt uncomfortable in her shorts and T-shirt and would willingly have discarded them but for Marlow's being there. She wished fervently that he would leave.

An hour passed. It was becoming a subtle torture to lie so close, aware that his glistening body lay within arm's reach. Out of the corners of her eyes she could see the firm bulge of his muscles, his torso curving away to his narrow hips, the blatant brevity of his swimming-trunks leaving nothing to the imagination. She shifted her attention to the powerful thighs and long, perfectly shaped legs ending in strong, well-shaped feet. One toe twitched as he turned to look across at her.

'Feeling restless, Flame?' He must have been watching her unconscious scrutiny. Her startled glance met his. The suggestive undertone in the softly spoken words made heat search along the length of her body in a tell-tale wash of pink, to lodge somewhere in her groin. She turned her head irritably.

'Restless,' he judged as if it proved something. 'You could go for a swim to cool off.'

She didn't answer.

'What about it?'

'What?' Flame glanced across at Samantha and Britt, but Samantha was now wearing a Walkman and seemed oblivious to everything else, while Britt preserved a discreet lack of interest in the conversation of her employers.

'What about a swim?'

'Why aren't you working?' she demanded.

'Today's my day off.'

'I'm surprised they can do without you!'

'I'm only a phone call away.' Marlow indicated a receiver bulging out of the back pocket of the white trousers he had discarded. 'Besides,' he went on, 'Victoria's in charge.'

'I'm sure she is,' muttered Flame.

Marlow's glance was thoughtful. 'She seems to bother you more than she should. She knows her place, you know.' Then, as if bored at the prospect of what seemed to herald another round of petty wrangling, he swung his legs over the edge of the sun-bed and gripped her arm. 'Come on. In the water.'

'But I don't want——'

'Tough!' He yanked her to her feet.

'And I haven't got a swim-suit——'

'On a private beach? With your husband? Does it really matter?'

She stepped back. 'If you think I'm going to disrobe in front of you, Marlow Hudson——' she began.

'Hell's bells, I've seen you in the nude before!' he exclaimed. Then seeing the truculent expression on her face he gave a wicked laugh. 'So what? Preserve your modesty if you must.' And before she could move he picked her up in his arms and started to run with her to the edge of the water.

The drenching she received was complete. She sat up furiously in two feet of salt water, wriggling angrily as a wave washed over her as if to drive the point home. 'You horrible devil!' she shouted. A mixture of salt tears and sea-water stung her eyes. It reminded her so much of times of old.

Marlow was looking pleased with himself as he swam off, cleaving the water with smooth strong strokes that made her heart turn over with the beauty of just watching him. His gypsy-dark hair was slicked to his scalp, drawing attention to the stark symmetry of his face, and his oiled body appeared and disappeared in the rolling surf, as if inviting her to join him.

In the old days she would have done so, showering water in his face, tugging at his legs to up-end him, revelling in the teasing game of hide and seek as their bodies found and lost and found each other again. It had happened before. He had always teased and sported with her in a part childlike, part adult way, so that when they eventually made love it was a delicious mixture of innocence and sin. Now she was too full of bitter knowledge to pretend things could ever have an innocent aura.

She stood up and turned her back, wrenching her T-shirt over her head and then stepping out of her soaking shorts. She threw them down on the sand. It would be all the same to him whether she was nude or clothed. He had Victoria to contend with, and all his provocation just now was obviously nothing more than an attempt to betray her into yet another revelation of her primitive desire for him. Maybe it bolstered his ego to witness the continual evidence of her 'weakness'.

Gloriously naked, she cut through the crystal water like a mermaid, her long hair streaming out behind her. She swam in the opposite direction to Marlow, darts of pleasure at the caress of the water against her naked skin recalling the sensuality of his touch warning her, as if she needed warning, of the dangers that lay ahead.

She swam far out, keeping as far away from him as she could, revelling in the sensual pleasure of sun and sea and her own nakedness. Above her head the sky was a dreamy blue. She floated on her back, kicking out her legs, then letting them float to the surface. Rollers lifted her and rocked her till she felt she was one with the elements. Suddenly she saw a dark head break the water beside her.

It was Marlow. He dived powerfully below the surface and came up underneath her, his arms sliding round her waist, pulling her body sensually against his own until she felt the familiar hardness with a shock of recognition. Without being able to stop herself, she felt her own limbs undulate against his before being caught up so that they became entwined as one. Her chin tilted to take a gasp of air before the surf laced over the tops of their heads. It swept them powerfully in towards the beach.

'Marlow!' she gasped, twisting in his arms as the surf rolled them over and over. 'Marlow——!' But his lips came down over hers as line after line of surf engulfed them. When they were flung free for a moment they were both breathless, and she knew it was more than the sea controlling them.

Before she could fight from out of his embrace the surf pounded on to the beach again, sweeping them both high up on to the sand. When it receded, Marlow was looking down at her with a hand planted on either side of her face. She arched back in the warm sand, then closed her eyes as she felt his thighs come down, pinning her beneath him.

Her bare feet kicked out, but to no avail. He was too strong, too purposeful. Eyes snapping wide, they dilated as she saw the dark head lowering, blocking out the sun, then his lips were covering hers, his tongue probing saltily into her half-open mouth.

It was a kiss that began slowly, almost reluctantly, but some demon of desire seemed to come alive at the same moment for them both, and, though Flame tried to tell herself she was writhing to free herself, when he lifted slightly her hips raised to follow, driven by more than anger.

'They'll see us,' she blurted when her mouth was released for a moment as he moved lower down to kiss her naked breasts.

'Is that all that's stopping us?' he demanded huskily.

Her eyes shot emerald sparks. 'Of course not!'

'No? I rather hoped it was...' he gave a wicked smile '...seeing they all left about five minutes ago.'

'What?' Flame tried to curve her neck so she could look up the beach, but it only gave Marlow an opportunity to trail a fever line of kisses along it. She could feel his tongue, his teeth, and now his hands everywhere. Even as her own body arched in response to his increasing ardour she heard herself say over and over, 'No, Marlow, please don't, don't please...' Then he stopped the broken words with his lips again and she felt her limbs turn to a blaze of gold like the sand on which they were lying and the sun which was caressing them from above.

When she seemed to be approaching the point of no return she felt him pause and raise himself on his hands to look down at her. 'At this point,' he said, half humorously, 'you should be saved by the sound of a helicopter flying overhead.'

'Would a thing like that stop you?' she asked, trying to make her tone as biting as possible. To her own ears it merely sounded like a reproach, but he took it the way she intended.

'It's only you yourself who's stopping me,' he rasped. 'I don't intend to force you to submit to something you'll later claim you never wanted. That's not my plan...' He gave a twisted smile. 'It never was and never will be.'

He rolled to one side, pulling her against him so that she lay within the crook of his arm. His voice was resonant as he growled down, 'I told you I wanted you, body and soul. And that's what it comes down to. What I want I get. And nothing less will do.'

His free hand began to fondle one of her breasts, but his touch was different, showing he had decided that he had gone as far as he would allow himself to go just then.

Relief was mixed with the inevitable regret in Flame's heart, but she knew her recent anger was light years away at this moment. She allowed him to go on holding her, knowing she would let him do whatever he liked with her—and smarting at the thought that he didn't guess how much he was in control.

If only he realised the truth, she thought, as time swelled, seeming to hold them inside an everlasting golden bubble. He has held my soul captive since the first moment we met, she reminded herself. If only the magic could work both ways and he would be an equal in love.

She had to be content that he held her now as if he cared, like a lover, like a husband, and they stayed like that until eventually, from the top of the cliff, came the sound of the gong summoning them to lunch. It was a signal from outside, bursting their unexpected dream-bubble and casting them out into the real world again.

Marlow pulled her to her feet without looking at her. She thought he seemed angry about something now as he walked her back in silence up the beach. But then he was often abrupt these days, for reasons she couldn't even guess at, and she was scorchingly aware how she had never really got to know him properly.

His life before he came to Santa Margarita was a closed book to her. Somehow there had never been time, or need, to delve back into the past. She hadn't got one. And his had never been an issue. Besides, everything had happened too fast. The miraculous thing that was their suddenly flowering love had stolen all their attention. And now, she realised with a tinge of regret, she had just thrown away the perfect opportunity to get him to unlock some of his secrets for her.

She trailed back beside him, trying with difficulty to realign her more ordinary everyday responses with the primitive urgings he had aroused but not satisfied.

CHAPTER SEVEN

AFTER lunch, when Samantha and Emilio had retired to their room and Britt had settled the children down for their own siesta, Marlow made his way to Flame's side. Having carefully avoided him since their interlude on the beach, she had no intention of being left alone with him just yet, not with everybody else out of the way. So to his suggestion to come and give her room the once-over to see if anything needed doing to it before she moved in, she shook her head.

'I won't come now if you don't mind. I want to go and have a chat with Mother. I haven't seen much of her today.'

'That won't take long—talking tires her at the moment. I'll come with you, then we can go on from there.'

'What about your siesta?' she asked, still trying to get out of being closeted alone until her emotions had been schooled back into place. Even just standing next to him was making her imagination run riot.

'You should know me,' he told her with a sardonic lift of his head. 'Since when have I needed an afternoon sleep?'

'With your late night last night I should have thought you'd welcome it,' Flame replied at once, trying to ignore the betraying blush that plainly showed she remembered the siestas they themselves had shared.

He didn't answer, nor did he take any notice of her obvious desire to be left alone. He held the door of Sybilla's room to let her go in ahead of him. The invalid was sitting up now, still flushed, but obviously well rested.

'You're a tonic, Flame, you really are!' She lifted her fadedly pretty face to include Marlow. 'Don't you agree, darling? I am looking better, aren't I? And it's all due to Flame coming back to us.' She reached out for their hands. Flame made sure she was standing on the opposite side of the bed to Marlow before she took it, but even at that safe distance she could feel the pulsing attraction of his physical presence reaching out towards her.

She sat down on the edge and he did likewise on the other side. Then he reached over and took her other hand in his and trapped it there on top of the coverlet. Trying to behave like the perfect loving husband, she registered, trying to disguise the wild starts of pleasure his touch wrought. Their hands lay entwined on the bed—like a visible lie. Her mother seemed to be quite taken in.

'I knew you two would get back together,' she was saying in a weak though happy voice. 'The shame is that it took so long. But let's not dwell on the past. It's now that counts.'

Marlow played up to the image of the attentive husband for the next twenty minutes, and Sybilla unconsciously egged him on, smiling from her daughter to her son-in-law, with such obvious happiness that Flame began to seethe at the game Marlow was forcing her to play.

Eventually he remarked that he and Flame were going to discuss the furnishings at the *casita*, and Sybilla patted

their hands with a little smile. 'I still get rather worn out
with too much talking... Go now—but don't forget to
come back and tell me what you've decided. I expect
you'll be thinking about a second bedroom?' She closed
her eyes, so missing Flame's startled glance.

'*Second* bedroom? Does she guess how things are
between us?' she demanded when they were outside.

Marlow's lips gave a sardonic twitch. 'Not in that
sense. Knowing your mother, she's hoping the second
bedroom is going to be done out in fluffy rabbits and
bows.'

It took a second for his meaning to sink in. 'Not on
your life!' she exclaimed. '*Us?*'

'Don't you want a family, Flame?' He walked on
ahead without waiting for her answer.

She caught up with him. 'Ignoring all that,' she
flounced her shoulders, 'surely you didn't have to go all
out to make it look as if you're the——' she faltered
'—as if you really care?' She turned when they were more
safely out of earshot. 'No wonder she's got us planning
nurseries, with you behaving like a doting husband!'

Marlow carried on walking without turning and she
ran after him again. 'It seems so underhand,' she said.
'Poor Mother, I feel I'm cheating her by letting her
believe everything's all right. Not that that would bother
you!'

'Do you think she's fooled? Or is she merely hoping
against hope? She's a shrewd woman, your mother,
Flame. She's nobody's fool. I think perhaps you
underestimate her.'

'Why else would she be so pleased with herself,' she demanded, 'if she didn't think we were both genuinely starry-eyed?'

'She ought to be pleased. She's beginning to recover from a serious illness. She's every right to be pleased.'

'And that's another thing, I should have been told she was so seriously ill. How dare you conceal something like that from me?'

Marlow frowned. 'In retrospect I agree with you. But as I've already told you, I didn't want to worry you unnecessarily, nor did I want her made even more upset by your sudden reappearance. Naturally I couldn't be sure you were going to behave yourself.'

'How *dare* you?' exclaimed Flame.

'Well, it's true.'

'I'm not a *child*!'

'You were when you left me.' He gave her a piercing glance. 'And sexual experience doesn't add up to maturity. You're still a child.'

'You can always be counted on to be patronising, Marlow Hudson!' she snapped, wanting to hit him.

He slid an arm around her waist. They had reached the pines that shielded the *casita* from the main house. She smelled the sharp scent of them. It had the tang of good bubble bath. Marlow let her go at once as soon as he'd made her stop. 'Tell me, Flame, am I too old for you?' His voice was quiet, with a gravity she was unused to.

She considered this unexpected question with her head on one side. Just to feel him near set her pulses racing. What had age to do with a thing like that? 'How? Too old?' she asked with a catch in her throat.

'I mean, you might feel you haven't had enough of discos and beach parties and all the razzmatazz of being crazy and irresponsible. I mean—hell, you're still only twenty, and here I am expecting you to talk to me about soft furnishings! Maybe you'd rather be chatting about pop groups or something?' His eyes were very still as if he didn't want to miss a millisecond of her reaction.

'I don't think I've ever been more than averagely mad about that sort of thing,' she told him. 'Discos?' She shrugged. 'I don't rule them out, they're fun. But they're hardly the centre of my existence.'

'What is the centre?' He frowned. 'Was it your job? Do you resent me for dragging you away from that?'

'I don't think that was central to my life. Not entirely,' she hedged.

She felt a lump in her throat and her eyes began to smart. Desperate to conceal the fact of tears, she dashed his hand away, spinning abruptly, and without a word, for words wouldn't come just then, she began to run along the path towards the house. Her action must have taken him by surprise, for she had time to reach the front and run round to the little flower-filled terrace at the back before he came out of the wood.

When he found her she was sitting on a bench and the face lifted to the sun was carefully schooled. It looked as smooth and untouched by emotion as a terracotta statue.

'You look like a sun goddess.' He hesitated, then sat down beside her. His tone was careful and conversational as if he wasn't sure what he wanted to say. 'Do you want to stay out here for a while?' He paused. 'There's no urgency about the furnishings. I take this weather for granted, but you must be feeling sun-starved after all that time in England.'

She felt his eyes on her but didn't open her own. 'What are you going to do this afternoon?' she asked.

'I take it that means you'd rather I disappeared?'

When she didn't answer he got up. 'I'll fix a drink.'

Flame heard him go inside. It was difficult after he'd gone not to ponder on his words in the pinewood, though she would rather not have had to face the further confusion they brought.

She looked down at her feet in their white sandals. They were half covered in pine needles. A thick carpet covered the path. It was soft and where her feet sank in she could feel more softness beneath. She considered her answer carefully.

If she blurted out what her centre was, she would have nowhere left to hide. Her humiliation would be complete. Marlow would know he had won more than just Cabo Santa Margarita.

She felt something warm on her neck. It slid beneath her chin and lifted her face. The tingling in her too sensitive skin told her it was his touch, feather-light, before her mind registered the fact of his fingers lifting her face to study it. She closed her eyes in order to shut out the blaze of blue that lasered over her face. How could he not see that she loved him? Why could he not love her in the same way? Why did everything have to be the way it was?

As if he could read something of her thoughts he said softly, 'It doesn't have to be a game of hurting, you know. I want you to be happy.'

'Happy?' Her voice cracked. How could she be happy when he had only married her to get his hands on their land ... and when he loved another woman? She wondered if he realised how close to the edge of hysteria he was pushing her. This teasing, taunting softness was worse than indifference, because it gave her hope when common sense told her there was none.

Why had he tried to make her believe he thought the problem between them was to do with discos and pop singers? It was as if he was trying to make her think she was the one who had broken things up between them. Then she had another thought. Maybe what he had said was a backhanded way of telling her she bored him. And that was why he had sought consolation elsewhere. Certainly Victoria was older and presumably more mature than she was, and somehow she couldn't imagine her giving two hoots about discos.

Maybe that was what he had meant. Maybe she was simply too gauche for him? That was why he'd gone astray in the first place: he had been trying to explain in as tactful a way as possible why he preferred Victoria. That must be it. Flame wondered what she could do about that. If she had wanted him back, of course, she would now show how sophisticated she could be. But she didn't want him, not even in this guise of gentle concern, because she knew it was fake.

Her misery made her rub a sticky hand over her sun-goddess face. Damn him, she thought, why did he switch on the charm just when she was beginning to gain some control? If he behaved like a first-rate louse all the time it would be easy to train herself to hate him as he deserved. But when he turned vulnerable, as he had done this morning in the kitchen, and started to talk as if he cared for her happiness, what was she supposed to do? She was only human, and it made her squirm to feel that her emotions could be used against her like this.

The trouble was he was too expert for her, too cynical, too sophisticated. And this he obviously knew. He'd done too much and knew too much, especially how to handle the opposite sex. He still knew the exact chord to strike, now hard, now soft, to get her falling head over heels for him.

He brought out two long drinks with plenty of ice chiming sharply against the sides of the glasses. He'd even iced and sugared the rims.

'Like a professional barman,' Flame observed, lifting the glass to her lips.

'I was a barman,' he smiled, and because she seemed to have given him an opening he sat down again beside her and said, 'Did you know I started to work my way around the world when I was seventeen?'

She recalled what Samantha had told her, but let him go on. 'Barman was just one of the jobs I had.' He looked down at her and thoughtfully wiped away a smear from her nose. 'You know very little about me really, Flame. When I was your age I'd already done a hell of a lot. By comparison you've led a very sheltered life— I forget that sometimes.' He gazed into the distance. When he looked down at her he gave a quick smile. 'I've got a lot of stories I could tell you. Bedtime stories, maybe?' He laughed, his eyes somehow shadowed. 'We never seemed to have time for that sort of thing before, did we? Just sitting talking.'

'With a six-week courtship? Plus the big fact that you're a workaholic? You scarcely had time for a honeymoon.' His touch had made her tremble, but she could still sound unmoved.

'Is that what you used to feel?' He seemed to ponder for a moment, then said, 'I guess I may have taken you a little bit for granted.'

'I——' she shrugged, surprised that such a thing wasn't beneath his consideration. He sounded as if he'd actually considered her! She wished he wasn't such a convincing actor. 'I actually had no expectations of any sort,' she told him, trying not to let him see her confusion. 'I'd never been married before and never given the matter much thought. It just seemed to happen. So I've no opinion about whether you took me for granted or not.'

'I should have given you more time.'

'Marlow,' she turned to him, her eyes luminous with the struggle taking place inside, 'you're not keeping your side of the bargain, are you?' And when he raised his eyebrows she explained, 'I said I'd stay with you for six months on the understanding that you were honest with me. I know why you married me—it's no use your trying to pretend otherwise. I know a lot of things you no doubt wished I didn't. So, although I appreciate your charm and the fact that you're taking time out to talk to me like a human being, I really do wish you'd stop treating me like an idiot. I know you don't care about me, not deeply, in the way——' She hesitated, about to say, in the way she wished, but corrected herself in time and went on, 'You don't care deeply in the way husbands do. Luckily,' she paused, 'it shouldn't matter much, should it?'

She glanced away, then pivoted back, determined to make him understand. 'What matters,' she said, 'is that you don't expect me to swallow a lot of gooey nonsense about love. We don't have to pretend with each other. There's no one to overhear us. We can be ourselves.'

Marlow was silent for so long she wondered if he had understood what she was saying after all. His face wore that blank look, like a mask, with only the bright, alive look in his eyes showing he was doing a lot of thinking. They were rather shadowed now, as if he didn't like what he was hearing.

He turned to her, a frown beginning to appear on his forehead. 'You'd like it straight, would you? Sex without love? I know we're agreed that the desire, or should I say the lust, is still there. But are you *sure* that's what you want?'

For some reason Flame felt herself go very still.

'All right,' he went on without changing his tone, 'take your dress off.'

'What?' Before she could move he reached out with one hand, his fingers groping into the top of her sun-bodice, and with an exclamation he yanked it open. Then his dark head bent to taste the honey beneath. Her hands came up involuntarily to push his head away, but the moment her fingers sank into the gypsy-black hair and she felt the thick strength of it running beneath her fingertips she felt them tighten, holding him against her for a moment, desiring nothing more than to bury her face in the darkness.

She let her eyes close, drinking in his presence, before she was able to assert her will. 'I *don't* want it to be like this——' she croaked.

Marlow's answer was to slide a hand beneath the hem of her skirt and let his mouth take her lips in a searing kiss that robbed her of breath. Twisting in his arms, she tried to protest as he lifted her up and began to carry her inside. The more she struggled, the tighter he held her.

When he had hauled her as far as one of the doors and paused to open it, she tried to slither away, but he was too strong for her, and she found herself in his arms again before landing in a confusion of limbs and amber hair on something soft.

It was the bedroom, she registered, Marlow's big double bed. He noted the widening of her eyes with a smile of savage humour. There was a ripping sound as he tore her skirt from waist to hem, and as she tried to wriggle away he caught her long hair and coiled it round one of his hands, forcing her head back with taunting gradualness until she was spread-eagled across the bed beneath him.

'You prefer it like this, darling Flame? Why ever didn't you say so?' he rasped as she vainly fluttered like a winged creature under the movements of his hands.

He was just about to unbuckle his belt when the extension phone beside the bed gave a bleep. The look on his face showed that he was going to ignore it, but as it continued he gave a gesture of irritation and reached out a hand. Flame should have been able to take the opportunity to escape, but he foresaw what was in her mind and increased his hold on the long loops of hair, wedging one knee across one of her thighs so that she was effectively trapped.

'Yes?' he barked into the mouthpiece. 'Oh, Victoria,' she heard his voice warm.

Only his own side of the conversation was audible, a series of yeses and nos, and then, 'Do you want me to come over?'

The answer was obviously affirmative and he replaced the receiver with a crash. 'You've got a temporary reprieve, darling,' he intoned. 'Make the most of it!'

He got up and went out. Flame stayed where she was for a moment, too numbed by the events of the last few minutes to do anything else. Then she sprang off the bed and pulled her torn clothing together as best she could.

Marlow was already shrugging into a bleached linen jacket, a briefcase lying open on his desk, as she walked past the door into the garden. She wanted to leave and never set eyes on him again, but something forced her to stop when she reached the path. Instead of walking out she went over to the low wall on the edge of the terrace, and when he was ready to go he found her there.

'I'm having to go down to town,' he called.

Flame pretended to be interested in the little blossoms of hibiscus scattered on top of the wall.

'Flame?'

'Yes, I heard.' She didn't look at him. He came to the edge of the terrace.

'Flame?' He waited until she looked up. 'I *have* to go.'

'Go to hell for all I care!'

'I don't think I'm going to do that. What I shall do is come straight back here where you'll be waiting for me.' He gave a confident smile and, looking handsome and sure of himself, moved to the edge of the terrace. 'I'll see you soon.'

'No doubt,' she replied easily, as if it didn't matter in the least.

With a growl of impatience Marlow strode quickly down the steps towards her and was by her side in a moment, sweeping her powerfully into his arms, hands feverishly searching out the familiar intimate places and, despite her feelings, thrilling her to feel him take possession of her. For one ecstatic moment time seemed to be stilled as they swayed in each other's arms. His mouth was hot as it covered her own, then he was disentangling himself from her arms. 'Mustn't get too carried away,' he crisped. 'It's only lust. And besides,' he offered a cynical smile, 'I don't want to keep Victoria waiting—she can be so impatient!' Then, with a world-weary lift of the hand, he was gone.

When she had seen him disappear round the side of the house Flame went back to studying the torn petals between her fingers. So much for his fine words about body and soul! she thought viciously. Straight sex was all he wanted every time. This was the truest thing he'd ever told her—and even that was presumably because even he couldn't conceal the physical evidence of his arousal! Now she imagined him speeding heatedly towards the willing lips of his mistress.

As soon as she heard the sound of the car fade into the distance she threw away the flower-heads she had been tearing into little pieces and gave full vent to her true feelings in the solitude of the garden.

CHAPTER EIGHT

MARLOW hadn't returned by the time Flame went to change for dinner. She knew he expected her to move her things to the *casita*, but the thought of being alone with him through the long hours of the night made her hesitate. She dared not think what might have happened if he hadn't received an urgent call.

Samantha popped her head round her bedroom door just as Flame was hanging everything back in her wardrobe and asked if she wanted any help.

'I'll wait awhile,' blurted Flame. 'It's cosier over here with you and the children. And if Marlow is going to be in the town all the time I'd rather be across here.'

Her sister covered her surprise. 'It's early days, I suppose.' She gave her an understanding smile, and Flame felt she ought to explain how he had been called out even though it was supposed to be his day off.

'Supper in an hour, then. We don't wait for Marlow if he's working in town, but he has all his meals over here when he's working in the *casita*.'

'Very convenient for him,' murmured Flame.

'You should understand one thing, Flame,' Samantha came in and held the door half closed, 'he's more than generous about household matters. At least give him credit for taking such good care of Mother.'

'But she doesn't need the sort of help you're referring to,' objected Flame. 'I'm sick of hearing from everyone

138

how good Marlow is! To me it sounds like charity, and I would have thought none of us had need of that.'

'You have a very bitter way of looking at things these days. You never used to be like this. It's London that's changed you, isn't it?'

'Of course not. And you should know the right answer. It was Marlow—he made me grow up.'

Samantha gave an exasperated sigh. 'Maybe you'll sort it all out in your head one of these days.' She went over to the bed. 'Is this the dress you're going to wear tonight?'

'No, I was just putting it away.'

Samantha fingered the pale cream silk. 'Wear it— you'll look gorgeous! I'll get changed too. Let's make a real occasion of it. We haven't really given you a proper welcome home.'

Flame tried to smile. 'All right. Dressing-up time!'

She knew she looked sophisticated in the cream silk— older, more assured—but she refused to dwell on why it mattered.

It was less than twenty minutes later when Flame emerged on to the terrace. Emilio, looking smart in a grey suit, had obviously been tipped off by his wife to don something vaguely dressy. Despite this he was wrestling with the barbecue, sleeves slightly rolled to avoid spoiling. He wasn't alone, however. Flame's glance was drawn to the tall, dark-haired figure helping him. It was Rafael.

He turned as soon as he heard her and came towards her with one hand outstretched. There was a large file lying open on the table, she noticed. He took one of her

hands in his, planting a very Spanish kiss on the back
of it before letting it go.

'You look quite dazzling, Flame. I trust things were
all right with you last night after I left? Samantha warned
me that I was being tactless.' His bright brown eyes
searched hers for hidden meanings, but she averted her
glance, Marlow's warning making her feel
uncomfortable.

'You know how it is. I've only just come home——'
she said feebly.

'And the relationship is still a little shaky?' He smiled.

'I'm sure we can solve our problems,' she blurted,
rather irritated that he should imagine he knew all about
her and Marlow's difficulties.

'I'm sure you can.' Rafael bent his suave head and
she caught a tantalising whiff of cologne. At that
moment Emilio went inside for something and Rafael
took the opportunity to move closer, but it was only to
tell her his reason for coming over this evening. He
indicated the file for Emilio, adding inconsequentially,
'But I understand I've been invited to dinner. A rather
special occasion, *no*?'

Flame opened her mouth to say something, then
thought better of it. Emilio must have invited him, being
quite oblivious, no doubt, to the drama that had gone
on underneath the surface last night. She gave him a
polite smile.

'That'll be nice. Perhaps if you're staying I can get
you a drink?' It would send her indoors so she could
ask Samantha what was going on.

She found her sister in the sitting-room, already
pouring gin and tonics. 'Marlow's going to be delighted

when he finds us dining in a cosy foursome. What on earth made Emilio invite him to stay?'

'He didn't realise.' Samantha grinned. 'The silly love has just told me—that's husbands for you! Still, I can ring round and ask one or two more people over. Here,' she thrust two glasses into Flame's hands, 'I'll do it now before it's too late.'

Flame saw her begin to riffle through a heavy address book. 'Don't worry,' she mouthed as she quickly punched in the first call and the phone began to burr, 'there's safety in numbers.'

With a glance Flame went outside again. Samantha liked nothing better than social crises. Sometimes Flame wondered if she engineered them, aided by Emilio's quite obvious lack of guile. At least Emilio's openness made a change from the deviousness that seemed to be Marlow's stock in trade.

She couldn't help wondering what he was doing at this moment, an unbidden image of him entwined in Victoria's welcoming arms blasting through her with a stomach-wrenching blow that momentarily stopped her breath. Taking a grip on herself, she forced herself to shut out the image and think of something else.

Rafael was making himself useful near the barbecue. He looked up when Flame reappeared and took the drink she offered with a quizzical tilt of his head. 'To your happiness, Flame. Welcome home.' There was a rueful twist to his lips and a sudden moment when the stillness between them spoke volumes of the regret he obviously felt.

'To your happiness too.' Her voice faltered and she bit her lip, wary of the special intimacy he seemed to want to force on her by his obvious show of interest.

He put a hand out as if to smooth a tendril of hair from her bare shoulder. 'I understand how things are. See me as a port in a storm—no strings. It's good to have friends.'

Flame blinked. Obviously he knew all about Marlow and Victoria. He wanted her to trust him—his eyes told her so. But she didn't want to take it any further. And her eyes, she hoped, told him that.

Then she felt something like a trickle of ice down her spine. A silent figure had appeared in the french windows. He stood without moving until she felt she could bear his controlled tension no longer. Stumbling forward, she nearly knocked Rafael's glass from out of his hand, but recovering, she hurried forward a couple of paces, before stopping again, her eyes glued to the expression on Marlow's face, guilt, she felt sure, engraved visibly on her own. But guilt for what? she thought furiously as she read the same impression in Marlow's ice-blue look.

'So we're having a party, Sam tells me. That's nice,' his voice grated with anything but pleasure. He came heavily down the steps with all the purpose of a man taking over. Flame felt branded as he moved his lips possessively and ostentatiously over her face before turning to their guest.

'Haven't I just seen you in town?' he asked in dangerously casual tones.

Rafael looked momentarily confused.

'I thought I saw you getting into your car as I drove up?' Marlow persisted, with a smile like an alligator.

'I guess you did. Sorry I couldn't stop.' Rafael licked his lips.

'No doubt you thought I'd be away longer than I was?' Marlow smiled easily as if there were no underlying meaning in what he was saying, but it was clear he thought Rafael had come straight out to see Flame as soon as he thought the coast was clear. He stood solidly between the two of them, almost blocking Flame out of the conversation. She moved round, bringing herself closer to Rafael than she meant to—but then, she thought, as she saw Marlow's expression, he had brought it on himself. It was all really too silly. Why did he keep pretending he was jealous? Would he lose face with other men if he allowed her too much freedom? It was pathetic—especially as he'd just come from the arms of his mistress. The thought made her want to be sick.

'I'll leave you two men to talk shop,' she said, tossing her long hair and giving them both a dismissive glance. Let them get on with it, she thought.

She fled indoors. 'Honestly, Sam,' she said crossly when she found her, 'those two are treating me like a piece of meat to be fought over!'

'How crude you are!'

'How insulting they are!'

Samantha was still busy at the telephone, but she held her hand on top of the receiver. 'Sure you're not enjoying your power? Rafael's a lovely man. Just the type to keep a husband on his toes—though perhaps that's the last thing you need at this point.'

'Sam, I'm exhausted by all this. Believe me! Why can't life be simple?' Flame clapped a hand to her mouth when she realised she was unconsciously quoting Marlow, though in a somewhat different context.

Later, as the last of the twenty or so guests Sam had managed to round up took their departure, her thoughts hadn't changed. It had been a pleasant welcome home with plenty of follow-up invitations, and the only cloud on the horizon was Marlow.

All evening he had watched her like a hungry panther eyeing its latest victim. It wasn't that he prevented her from talking to Rafael if she wanted to, it was just that his dark eyes followed her everywhere. She took care to avoid doing anything to inflame his suspicions, spreading her attentions equally among the guests, but Rafael watched her too, his eyes dark with lost opportunity. She hoped he could see she wouldn't welcome any further advances. It must be obvious to him that she had enough to think about, with Marlow brooding over her like a particularly dangerous predator.

When the last guest had gone she was alone on the terrace until a silky voice in her ear made her swivel.

'Ten out of ten for good behaviour!' Marlow slid an arm round her waist, dragging her violently against his taut body. When she was safely trapped in his arms he murmured, 'I've been wanting to do this ever since we were interrupted this afternoon.' He claimed her lips before she could reply, and she shivered in his arms.

'Cold?' He enveloped her more completely in his grip. But it wasn't the temperature, but the fact that the night lay ahead of them, the endless night hours . . .

The night was still warm, in fact, windless, and full of stars. He kissed the side of her forehead. 'We're not going in yet.' He lifted her fingers halfway to his lips as if about to kiss them, then, apparently thinking better of it, pulled her towards the stone steps leading up to the roof. At the top Flame couldn't restrain a little gasp. It was like a world of its own. Away from the lights of the house the sky was like an endless velvet tunnel leading straight to eternity.

'The Iroquois believe the stars are millions of pebbles thrown into the well of night by the gods in a game of chance,' he told her in a voice as soft as fate. 'Each star has written on it a separate destiny. There's you up there, and me...'

She was trembling now at the thought of their inevitable destiny, and allowed him to tuck her hand inside the pocket of his white dinner-jacket as he led her across the roof-terrace. Music was floating up from the valley. She felt faint under the tormenting caress of his thumb inside her wrist. Her whole body seemed to flame and her senses were more alive than ever, focusing on that one point of physical contact as if it were the pivot of the universe.

Before her knees quite gave way Marlow unfolded her hand from his pocket and pulled her down on to the cushions piled on the wide parapet, leaning back against the iron balustrade with his arms outstretched towards her. Then he drew her slowly down to him, his eyes black hollows, only his teeth gleaming as he murmured her name.

'You look like heaven in this cream silk, darling. Perfect with your butterscotch hair. How the hell I managed to keep my hands off you all evening——' His voice dropped a couple of intervals. 'You were driving me wild, did you know? Everybody could tell...'

Flame tried to control the crazy hammering of desire his words aroused, aware that he always had the power to mesmerise her when he wanted to with his husky voice. Now she could feel its power beginning to work on her again, though she tried to tell herself that words were cheap and that a man of his experience knew every trick in the book.

'It's late——' she began, irrationally trying to stave off the inevitable.

'I won't rush you...' He pulled her back, tracing a pattern over the back of the hand he had caught, and she saw his eyes glint like silver in the darkness.

'It was a nuisance having to break off so suddenly this afternoon,' he murmured. 'Though maybe things were beginning to get a bit out of hand. You drove me to say things I didn't mean. Bad luck I was called away...but at least it's given me a chance to cool down.' He paused. 'And maybe you've had a chance to think things over too...'

'It doesn't matter.' She turned her head so she didn't have to look at him. 'Business always comes first,' she said bitterly. He was trying to enchant her with his magic. Yet even knowing that, she felt helpless to resist. But she mustn't let him see that. Her heart was bumping rapidly, surely audible, a give-away to the effect of his nearness.

'This afternoon was a drag,' he frowned. 'It was something only I could handle, as it turned out.'

I bet! she thought, still trying to resist, once again imagining Victoria rippling with pleasure in his arms. But his voice was so softly persuasive she was almost tempted to give him the benefit of the doubt. Perhaps it had been work. Something urgent. His business interests were obviously colossal.

But it wasn't the first time things had been like this. And as he had so rightly said, it was only lust. And all it meant was that lies could be told in a voice no different from the voice of love.

When her head tilted and she gazed into his face she was surprised to see a nerve jump at the side of his mouth. Before she could surmise what sort of emotion it betrayed he said abruptly, 'Get to know me again, Flame. Relearn me.'

'How?' she blurted, her eyes widening a little.

'In every way possible,' he murmured, fixing her with his glance.

The warm heat of his body echoed the spoken invitation, bringing a shudder of desire slamming through her. To conceal it she pretended to look out across the tops of the trees below them, aware that he was deliberately trying to awaken her hunger for him, and trying to conceal how easily he could do it.

'I'd like to know you properly, Marlow,' she admitted with trembling lips. 'We never seemed to have time before.' She wondered if he knew how her control was hanging by a thread. She forced herself to go on. 'You've never talked to me about yourself. Never told me about your past.' She gave a grown-up little smile. 'I know you must have one.'

Her attempt to normalise the situation before they were swept to the land of no return seemed to work. Marlow gave a grimace and leaned back, but then he said, 'Don't you think you might have been upset by some of the things I could have told you?'

'Why do you put it in the past?' she frowned.

There was a seemingly endless pause before he said, 'I'm not likely to make the same mistake twice.'

'Mistake?' She raised her head.

'The mistake of imagining it's either necessary or desirable to be close to any other being on the planet.' His lips were two firm lines.

'But that's terrible!' she exclaimed. 'You must be so lonely...'

'Lonely?' He gave a harsh laugh. 'When the chips are down I've only got myself. You're different. You've always had a loving family behind you. You've never known anything else. Anyway,' he went on before she could interrupt, 'I'm not in the business of dredging up the past for anybody these days. It's not what counts.'

'What does count, Marlow?' Flame asked in a small voice. 'Success? Is that all that matters to you now?'

'You've got it in one, darling. Success, having things my own way. Having you.' His eyes glinted cynically and she longed for his former mood to return when they had begun to seem a little closer.

'What's the point of success,' she asked, 'if there's nobody to share it with?' When his only answer was an abrupt snort of derision she made an effort to recreate the intimacy of their former mood by asking, 'I don't know why you think I'd be upset by anything you have to say. As you've just told me, what's past is past.'

'You mean you'd like to hear about my former girl-friends?' Marlow raised an eyebrow.

'Maybe not all about them.' She bit her lip and gave him a shaky smile. 'But it's no good if there are secrets between us. Not if we're going to try to get through the next six months together.'

To her relief he leaned back, folding his arms behind his head. 'You're right, of course—we never have talked much. There was always too much else to do...' His eyes were liquid, full of other meanings, but seeing her expression he closed them and began, 'The past...it seems like a mirage now. There's nothing in my present life to compare with it. Thank heavens for that!' He opened his eyes and gave her a careful look.

'It couldn't have been all bad,' she observed, wondering if this was how he was going to avoid telling her anything about it.

'It wasn't all bad,' his voice was soft, 'there were little pockets of pleasure, challenges accepted and won. I'm not one of these people who live life with a heart full of regrets.' He leaned back again and let his eyes probe the stars above them, then with a smile suddenly playing around his lips he admitted, 'The first girl who ever kissed me was called Holly Cinnamon. I was fourteen and she was sixteen. She decided she wanted me and that was it. I was immensely flattered. And the first girl I ever gave my heart to was Helen Jones. We were both seventeen. When I ran away from home,' he went on, 'I had to leave her behind. At the time it seemed the worst part of it. But I'd decided I couldn't stay, so that was that.'

His glance swivelled as he felt her lean towards him. 'Why did you leave home?' she asked softly.

'Strictly speaking I ran away from school. They decided to pack me off to boarding school for the first time at the age of seventeen. I wasn't having that. I changed trains on my way there and went to the nearest port, lied my way on board a merchant ship as a deckie and got off some months later in the next port, which happened to be Rio. By then Helen Jones and everything else that had led me to leave was but a distant memory. I forgot everything except the rules of the game I found myself in.'

He grinned wickedly, almost defiantly then, so that Flame got a glimpse of the boy he might have been at seventeen. 'They were harsh rules,' he went on, 'but I was a fast learner. My God,' he exclaimed, 'I must have had lady luck on my side in those days! But I came through. I won. I survived. One thing,' he told her, becoming serious, 'I resolved never to let a son of mine go through an experience like that.'

He reached out for her hand. 'I had a lot of——' He hesitated. 'Well, you asked for it. I had a lot of women in those days. A girl in every port. I spent six years bumming around the world—trekked across China, touched down in Australia and Indonesia, made my way back to Europe eventually via Calcutta and Bombay. I've found there's always somebody around willing and eager to offer a bed to a lonely young lad on his own in return for a little loving kindness. Things have changed now, but in those days you didn't question it. You could take each day as it came with a quick prayer to your lucky stars for what they provided.'

When he paused Flame asked, 'What made you stop travelling if you liked it so much?'

'I found the climate here congenial,' he said, somewhat evasively. After a pause he added, 'I had an aversion to turning into the sort of drunken seaman you find in every port with nothing to call his own but a fund of anecdotes.' He paused again. 'Actually, my mother died.'

The silence grew, and she wondered if he was ever going to go on, but finally with a small grimace he admitted, 'They told me afterwards she'd been asking for me right up to the end. I never made it back in time...' He turned away, harsh-voiced as he said, 'The past is finished with. There's no going back. I decided then, though, that I was going to leave something behind. Make my mark.'

'You've done that now.'

'Sure...' his lips twisted '...I've done it. This bit of coast was nothing but bleak scrub and a few dying villages when I arrived. Now it's a thriving community. I've brought people back to the area. I've built a clinic, a school, a library. I've done what I set out to do.'

Despite his words the harsh lines on his face expressed dissatisfaction. 'I wonder if we can ever have it all?' he mused half to himself. He gave a world-weary shrug. 'I was brought up by my mother. We didn't live in poverty—not the sort of poverty I've since seen in certain parts of the world—but it was tough. Maybe because there were just the two of us we were very close. I resolved to leave school and get a really good job at the earliest opportunity. Then she remarried.' He frowned. 'At first I was overjoyed. She was happy—she deserved to be. But things didn't quite work out the way I hoped.

It wasn't that the man she married wasn't comfortably off. And he was generous to Mother. He obviously cared for her. But he couldn't stand having a young buck like me on his territory, making him feel old. The family I'd dreamed about through the years when I'd seen other kids with their brothers and sisters, uncles, aunts, grandparents—the little family threesome I thought I was going to be part of remained a dream after all. He wanted rid of me. So that was that.'

His eyes glinted silver in the moonlight, self-mocking, his lips lifting cynically. 'That's life... Now I've got all the wealth I used to dream of giving to my mother, but still that elusive thing—a family of my own—escapes me.'

Something Samantha had told Flame came to mind and she was forced to say in a small voice, 'But you belong here, Marlow. With us.'

He gave a far-away smile. 'I used to think that, because I knew I'd found the right girl at last. And I believed— I believed I would one day have children of my own.' He paused. 'I suppose I had some romantic notion of the family because it was something I'd never had. I thought I could have it at last.' He gave a harsh laugh. 'Unrealistic, wasn't I?'

His confession had captured her sympathies, ensnaring her soul in a way she hadn't expected, but a subtle sexual chemistry was also at work between them, and it was this that was leading her deeper down the path she longed to follow. Now, despite her attempt to remain indifferent, the fires began to flare brighter as he slipped an arm around her waist. She felt the slight abrasion of his chin against her cheek as he turned his head and began to press her to him in an increasing fever of longing.

Biting delicately at the lobe of her ear, he began to slide his lips down the silken column of her neck, then retracing his tracks to take her lips, bruising them with a sudden storm of kisses that made her breathless with the longing for more.

'I want you so much, Flame. Want me—show me again. I'll settle for six months if that's what it takes.'

Without giving her time to answer he brought his free hand skimming over her thigh, smoothing down the fine cream silk of her dress with the flat of his hand so that she could feel the heat of it through the thin material. The recognition of what it was doing to her made her cheeks glow with a soft sheen, and she squirmed as she felt a response like a fireball between her thighs. Her body began to arch towards him despite the hammering of her mind ordering her to resist.

Dragging her face away with an effort, so that only her neck was bared to the pressure of his lips, she tried to bend away, pushing at the taut muscles crushing her back among the yielding cushions. But by now her desire was evident in her shallow, rapid breaths, and Marlow murmured hoarsely against her cheek, 'You don't want to fight me... We don't need that, Flame. We can be so good to each other. Let me show you how. Come to me...'

He began to lift the hem of her skirt, centimetre by centimetre, his own breathing laboured now, warm breath fanning her heated skin. She felt his hand slide to the moist warmth beneath the froth of lace she wore, forcing an involuntary gasp of pleasure from deep within as he found and caressed her, making ripples of pleasure follow themselves in increasing waves up the length of her spine. Her breasts ached with a new fullness and she longed for him to touch them, to ease the burning need he was deliberately arousing.

It didn't seem to matter now that he was going to take everything she possessed. He was the only man she had ever loved. Maybe one day he would learn to love her with a similar self-destructive hunger, with a love that had no limit.

'We want each other,' he was murmuring, running his tongue tauntingly over her swollen lips. 'You try to pretend you don't want me, but despite yourself you can't resist.' His restless, taunting lips hovered over her mouth. 'You can't resist this...' His lips pressed down on her own sending shoots of pleasure through her. 'And this——' he murmured, touching the swelling tips of her breasts with his tongue. 'And this——' He moved his head lower, seeking the heated centre of her being. And then he lifted his head, saying, 'I could take you, Flame. I could have you now, and God knows I want to... But...' He paused, and the night was still and the stars silent above their heads.

Flame's breath caught in her throat. He looked so strong, shoulder muscles bulging as he supported himself above her, and with her head thrown back against the cushions on the stone parapet she knew she was expressing the state of abandonment to which he had brought her. But she saw his eyes like two slits of blue ice glinting through the veil of lowered lashes, and she tensed at what she saw in them, feeling, before he began to draw back, that he was going to desert her.

He was still hesitating, perhaps regretting the impulse that had led him to carry her to such a pitch of desire— she didn't know. But he was going to turn away from her; she could read it in his eyes. Panic at being deserted by him made her struggle up. He couldn't reject her. He mustn't! Her fingers feverishly reached for his face, tracing the hard line of his brow-bone, then tangling avidly in the thick dark hair, hunger too long unsatisfied shuddering through every nerve as she inexpertly tried to show him the depth of her need. He stilled her hands in one of his, a look of indecision hovering over his face.

'You want me...' He gave a slight groan and bit the tips of her fingers, crumpling them painfully in one hand as he leaned towards her. 'You always wanted me...but what does it mean?' he demanded. He released her hands and she trembled as his tormenting caress began to trace the jutting outline of her breasts, finding the hard peaks at once, possessing them in a sudden plunging of his head so that his mouth claimed them, moving from one to the other, licking and teasing them to quivering arousal again. His eyes darkened to indigo as his clutching fingers grasped folds of silk, ripping open the ribbon fastening of her dress so that it fell away in a ripple of cream silk.

His sudden coolness subsided under the raw heat of his primitive response at the sight of her naked body and he gave a sharp groan of helpless rage as their bodies twined together in unashamed hunger. 'I need you, Flame. You're my wife,' he muttered possessively against her swollen mouth. 'Give me what belongs to me. Give it to me, darling. You're mine. I need you...' His voice became a hoarse, demanding whisper that thrilled her as much by its urgency as by the words he used.

As she pulsed to the insatiable greed with which he demanded her response, his words aroused in her the tiny voice of reason, for his words echoed too with the greed of his insatiable empire-building. She knew why he wanted her. And it was nothing to do with love.

She tried in vain to argue herself into making one final effort to resist, but, despite herself, the liquid honey of his caresses numbed her last shred of resistance, and she moaned against him, clinging to the broad muscles of his back as he crushed against the pale form opening helplessly for him. Her glowing limbs spread beneath him in a luxury of surrender.

She was barely conscious of any other sound but the repetition of her name whispered urgently by the man leaning over her, but with her eyes wide, drinking in the gorgeous beauty of him, she saw first a beam of light, a spotlight, from somewhere out of the darkness down below as it lit up the muscular curve of his shoulders. Sight was quickly followed by sound with the thrumming note of a car labouring up the steep lane.

'Who the devil is this?' rasped Marlow, freezing in the act of lifting her pliable body into his arms. Melded together in stillness, they listened for the sound of the car as it drove at speed through the open gates. It came to a skidding halt in the courtyard below and light footsteps were heard running across the paving stones towards the *casita*.

'Someone for you,' said Flame dully, recognising at once the direction in which the footsteps were going. They were light steps too, those of a woman for sure. Her flesh crawled with apprehension.

'Hell and damnation, not now!' Marlow dragged her roughly against him.

A voice called from below, called his name. It was unmistakably a woman's voice.

'I'd better see what it's about.' Marlow released her with a show of reluctance and began to fasten the buttons of his shirt as he got up.

'Yes, go!' she cried in a sudden desperation, pushing at him so she could wriggle free from under his restraining weight before he could stop her. His body followed hers, dragging her against him, shirt still unfastened.

'Go!' she cried again, shaking off his hands. 'Go to her! You don't have to pretend—I know who it is! Go to her, Marlow. And don't ever touch me again!' In a storm of despair she flung herself away, pulling her dress closed as she fled across the roof to the steps.

'Flame, *wait*!' He followed, catching her round the waist as she reached the top. 'Why are you running away again? Are you going to do this sort of thing forever?'

'Why should I stay to be humiliated?' she bit out, grappling wildly with him, feeling his superior strength quell her feverish attempts to free herself.

'What humiliation? What are you talking about? You don't imagine it's some girlfriend, do you?'

'*Isn't it?*' She crouched in front of him like a wildcat.

'Let's go and see,' he suggested mildly, trying to calm her. His tone had lightened, at once fuelling her suspicions again, for how could he joke at a time like this, unless his feelings were totally under control? And if they were under control, what had the last few minutes of abandoned lovemaking been?

'You're coming with me.' He gripped her by the shoulder. 'Come on.'

Flame had no choice but to allow him to force-march her down the steps. At the bottom he slackened his hold, and she had time to retie the front of her dress and smooth her hair as she reluctantly followed him to the edge of the pine trees. A pale figure was already running back towards them. She felt Marlow jerk to a standstill, and his grip slackened. With a cry Victoria came running out of the trees and threw herself hysterically into his arms.

'Thank God you're here!' She was sobbing, her arms laced around his neck. Flame watched him hold her in his arms. He was murmuring something to her, but she couldn't hear what.

A hand of ice drew her back into the shadows. Marlow had already forgotten she was there. His head bent as Victoria lifted her face to his, and in a moment she was dragging him towards her car.

Something made him turn. 'Flame!' he called. 'I've got to go and sort something out...'

She couldn't bring herself to say anything. With a fixed expression she swivelled and made her way inside like somebody in a dream. Then she went to the bathroom, brushed her teeth, took a shower, being careful not to wet her hair, then went along to her room and, after undressing, lay down naked underneath the duvet.

Hours passed. She thought she heard voices outside, then nothing. Silence. Dawn came. Her eyes stared as if lidless at the window. A bird stood on the window-sill and sang its contribution to the dawn chorus, then it flew away. Flame still stared. Her face felt hot and dry as if she had a fever. Sweat trickled icily between her breasts, but she didn't care. Her limbs had been on fire; now they felt as cold as lead. She began to shiver. It was then that Marlow entered the room.

Before he could offer excuses she sprang up to sitting, taut as a bow, her face tight with pain. 'Don't tell me. It was work again. Night duty! Quite unavoidable. Just get out!'

'Flame, I can explain——'

'Don't waste your breath.' Her voice sounded as cold as death. 'I simply want to apologise for my performance on the roof. I'm sorry if I gave you the wrong impression. Actually the truth is I was missing Johnny, and I'm sure you know how it is—any port in a storm, as they say.' She gave a shaky laugh, wondering why he didn't say anything.

He was staring at her with eyes like hollow pits, made worse by the sudden blanching of his cheeks.

'I can see you're shocked. It must be a surprise to find you're not the only one who can put up a good act when the occasion demands.' Flame tried to give a little laugh. 'You see, I have learned something in London, contrary to what you thought.' She paused, striving to control her voice. 'I just wanted you to know,' she went on steadily, 'there's no need to come out with a trail of excuses. We agreed on truth, remember?' She raised her head. 'What's the matter?' she asked sharply. 'You're looking serious. It's only a *game*, Marlow. I hope you didn't take me seriously?' She gave another peal of laughter, more assured than the first. 'I know you're too sophisticated not to realise it's all a game.'

'You were *faking*?' His voice was scarcely audible.

'Not entirely. It was lovely, Marlow. Pity we couldn't finish the scene. Tell your girlfriends to time their entrances with more care in future. If there *is* a future,' she added.

He ignored that and demanded, 'Was it just sex with you? Has there never been anything more? I thought——'

'Don't worry, you don't have to feel guilty.' She gave a hollow laugh. 'I'm sure your ego can cope with the fact that I don't happen to be as besotted with you as *she* is,' she said, voice rising as she almost lost control again. She managed to force an artificial playfulness into it as she went on, 'As you can see, it doesn't matter a damn. We might even be able to have fun together when you've sorted out your other problems. Who knows?'

She gave an exaggerated yawn. 'I'm so sleepy. You are naughty for waking me up!'

She lay down and pulled the duvet over her face, knowing she couldn't go on any longer with the charade. Marlow's face had been wiped of any response and her own heart was thundering so loudly she felt he must be able to hear it.

She was a living wound. But she didn't know who she hated most, him or herself for allowing him to dupe her once again. If he doesn't leave my room soon I won't be able to hold on, she thought, biting her bottom lip so hard in order to stop herself from sobbing out loud that she tasted blood.

There was a slight sound, then a bang as she heard the door close. When she flung the covers back he had gone.

Aching in every limb, she stayed in bed until late that morning, eventually falling into a fitful sleep. During it she dreamed she was back on the roof with Marlow. They were arguing in a friendly fashion about something or other, and what he said made her run lightly to the edge of the roof. His shout made her spin as she teetered on the edge. Just before she plunged to the flagstones below he was beside her, crumpling her in his arms. 'It's a long drop,' he breathed, 'for heaven's sake be more careful!'

They clung to each other, and Flame knew he truly cared by the way he held her. She felt his heart beating hard against her own ribs and her own heartbeats increasing to match his. She wanted to tear aside the clothes that stopped them from touching each other, but when she unbuttoned his shirt there was another one underneath it, and when she tried again there was another one beneath that. 'Time to go,' he told her. 'I have to work.'

When she woke up her pillow was wet with tears.

CHAPTER NINE

FEELING bruised all over and wondering how a broken heart could show itself in such a totally physical way, Flame crawled outside just before lunch and collapsed behind a pair of dark glasses on one of the sunbeds. A lather of tinted sun-screen covered her tear-scoured cheeks, and by now she felt she had no more tears left.

At least it proves I'm still alive, she told herself fiercely, snatching at any small comfort she could find. While she was in London her feelings had been switched off, and she had sometimes wondered if she was doing permanent damage to her emotions by shutting down so completely.

Now she knew it had only been temporary. All she had been waiting for, it seemed, was for Marlow to come back into her life—Marlow, with his tortuous double-dealing—Marlow, with his soft lies that could wound worse than the most biting words ever spoken—Marlow, who alone of all the men she'd met could really make her feel... even if it was only like hell.

The children were splashing each other by the water's edge in a game that seemed to go on without sense or end. She tried not to let it get through to her, but there was something about their sweet babyness that made her own pain the harder to bear.

She remembered the look on Marlow's face when he'd pointed to her mother's desire to see the *casita*'s spare room do duty as a nursery. Now she saw with a painful stab that it had been what she secretly wanted all along.

The continual squeals of delight coming from the shallow end of the pool began to make her long to get out of earshot. Samantha was just as bad, and Britt too, both women laughing uproariously as they dunked the three little ones in turn into the pool. By rights she should have been with them, fulfilling the happy role of aunty.

She got up, disgusted by her own spinelessness. Perhaps if she had let rip with her true feelings for once, instead of pretending to be so hard-boiled, she wouldn't feel so bad now. But it wasn't in her nature to shout and rave. Her pride wouldn't let her wear her heart on her sleeve. She wouldn't allow Marlow the satisfaction of chalking up one more victory. Why should she?

She went restlessly indoors, intending to fix herself a drink. She smiled bitterly at the thought of drowning her sorrows. There was plenty of opportunity. But she wasn't about to let Marlow see her lose control.

She was brought to a halt beside the phone. In all that had happened she hadn't yet made that call to Johnny. Now she thought about it, maybe it had been for the best. For only yesterday she would have told him she thought it doubtful that she would be going back. Now, the more she thought about it, the more likely it was that she would be going back just as soon as her mother was strong enough.

An abrupt longing to hear his friendly voice again swept through her. There would never be any melodrama with Johnny. He was far too casual about everything to let anything bother him for long.

God, how she needed someone like that now! Someone to laugh her out of this black despair that had got her in its grip. Brushing aside the fact that Johnny hadn't actually helped her forget Marlow when she'd been working for him, she built up an idealised picture of his boyishly handsome face. He would take her in his arms and tell her what an idiot she was. And maybe this time, this time she might feel something... She looked at the phone again. He was only a call away. Then she paused, her hand actually touching the receiver. He would be busy right now. Instead she would ring him this evening before he left for home. Then they would have a nice long chat. It was a thought to help her through the day.

Without her realising it her senses were attuned to the sound of Marlow's return. He obviously wasn't at the *casita*, for his car was gone. But when he didn't appear at lunchtime she was compelled to ask Samantha where he was, surprised she could even say his name without spitting with fury or alternatively bursting into tears.

'Meetings in town. You know him, always busy.'

'I expect he is,' Flame said sarcastically before she could stop herself.

Samantha gave her a look. 'Call him if you want a word.'

'Maybe I will.' But she knew it wasn't true. Not if it meant having to go through his so-called assistant to reach him.

Somehow or other she managed to get through the long hours of the afternoon. While everyone slept she raided Marlow's bookcase and came up with a Raymond Chandler she hadn't read for years, but before she left the *casita* she looked round the sitting-room. It had an unused air, more like a hotel lounge than a home. Given the chance she could have made it into a cosy retreat for them both. If only, she thought. If only he'd been different! She went out hurriedly, slamming the door firmly behind her.

At half-past five, still with the book in her hand, she went to the phone in the kitchen. Samantha and Emilio were on the terrace, so she couldn't use the one in the sitting-room in case they overheard her. For some reason she didn't care for them to know who she was ringing. They would demand explanations she couldn't give.

'Johnny?' She got through straight away. 'It's me.' And when there was silence at the other end she added, 'Flame. I'm ringing from Spain.'

'Flame, sweetie!' Johnny sounded surprised. 'So how's it going? Made it up?'

'You have to be joking! It's even worse than I imagined.'

'Poor baby! The man needs his head examining. But it sounds good from this side. You must be thinking of coming back?'

'If you'll have me——' she said, biting her lip at the obvious double meaning.

'I'll have you any time,' came the predictable response.

Flame laughed. Johnny was so safe because she always knew what he was going to say next, and his easy sympathy was balm to her battered soul. 'Johnny, I've really missed you,' she said, meaning it. 'Things have been really heavy here—I can't tell you what it's been like.'

'Listen, baby, I'm just on my way out to—er—a meeting, you know.' He gave a little laugh. 'Can't hang about, you know how it is. But let me know what time and date you're arriving and I'll try to get to the airport to meet you.'

'Same old Johnny,' she said, not at all jealous that he clearly had a date with someone else. 'You are sweet. I'll do that. It'll be heaven to see you!' She didn't mean heaven exactly and he knew that. It was the way he talked and she had always picked up on it.

'See you soon, then, baby. Take care—love you.'

'Love you too, Johnny.' Love meant something undemanding to Johnny, something that could be spread around, with no hassle if things didn't work out. Flame picked up on that too. It was a relief to de-energise the word, relieving it of all the agonising connotations it had acquired with Marlow.

She replaced the receiver, not happy, but her pain temporarily eased by the prospect of escape.

'It'll be heaven to see him, will it?' a voice thick with sarcasm broke into her reverie.

She spun with a gasp. Marlow himself was standing in the doorway, his face like nothing she had ever seen before. His skin wasn't white so much as colourless. It was anger that made him look like that, she supposed. But why should he be angry, having spent the rest of the previous night and presumably most of today with his mistress?

She drew herself up. 'Absolute heaven,' she agreed. 'I told him I was going back.'

'So I heard.' He took a pace into the room. 'When?' His voice was like the sound of wind through dry reeds.

'I don't know. Soon. As soon as I can. Why?'

'Why?'

'Will it cause too many problems for you, Marlow? Surely you've got the lawyers in your pocket too? Marcos, Rafael—surely they'll fix things so you get what you want after all, without having to go through the hassle of being married to me?'

'Hassle? I didn't know you went in for understatement. Judging by your phone conversation——' Marlow broke off as if he couldn't be bothered to finish what he had been about to say, running a hand through his gypsy hair. 'Maybe you weren't overstating the case just now?' He narrowed his glance. 'Maybe you do love the guy. What's he like?' He moved closer. 'Come on, Flame, tell me. What's he really like, this lover boy in London?'

He suddenly moved right across the kitchen and seemed to loom over her, but he didn't lay a finger on her and she clenched her fists, determined not to be cowed by his dark rage.

'Johnny?' She pretended to think. 'Well, he's good-looking. Tallish. Fair to mid-brown hair, sort of spiky. Grey eyes... Nice.'

'Nice?'

She nodded. 'Yes, he's a nice guy. He makes me laugh.'

'He makes you laugh?'

'I don't know why you keep repeating everything I say. What's it to you what he's like? I don't go around cross-questioning you about Victoria.'

'What the hell is this about Victoria? She's a business colleague, goddamn it!'

Flame flinched at the casual lie, more saddened than she would have thought possible that even now he refused her the truth. 'Of course she is,' she said tiredly. 'Just a workmate.'

Suddenly his anger seemed to erupt. 'What the hell are you accusing me of? What is all this?'

'Keep your voice down,' she hissed. 'Mother will overhear!'

'*Damn——*' Marlow broke off and with an immense effort clenched his jaw. She could see his face muscles bulge with the effort. 'We're going somewhere where we can talk.' His hand shot out to grip her by the arm.

'I don't want to——'

'To hell with what you want! If you intend to leave soon you can damn well give me what *I* want for a change!' He tugged at her and she staggered forward into his arms. 'And you know what I want, don't you, Flame?' he rasped dangerously, dragging her even closer.

Scratching at his face didn't help and, still protesting, she found herself being hauled across the kitchen. Now mainly concerned about the painful grip in which he held her, she cried, 'I don't want bruises!' whispering her protests as he hauled her along. The book she had been reading had fallen to the floor and he scooped it up with a glance at the title before flinging it on to the table. Then he opened the kitchen door and proceeded to bundle her through it.

'You're bruising me!' she protested again in the corridor, wriggling in vain.

'You'll have some explaining to do to lover boy, will you?' His eyes were storm-blue, bleak as an arctic sea.

'Bruises on your arm are innocent enough. Wait till you get them elsewhere on your anatomy!'

'Don't threaten me——' she began helplessly, trying to pull away again.

'Shut up, you'll have everybody coming to see what's happening!'

'Let me go, then, you heel!' she whispered furiously.

Marlow released her arm only when he'd extracted an agreement to go over to the *casita* with him without a struggle. Even so he kept a vicious hold on her, making her stumble once or twice when she couldn't keep up as he hauled her along. His anger was violent and seemed entirely genuine. But Flame was past trying to make sense of him. All she could think was that she'd bottled things up for too long and now she was going to have the chance to get everything into the open at last. Almost everything, she thought, squeezing her eyes tight. She allowed him to drag her across the garden to the pinewood and on through the trees to the little house beyond.

Then he flung open the door and pushed her inside. He went at once to the drinks cabinet and poured himself a triple Scotch. 'Want one?'

'Not that much.'

He took no notice and poured the same measure into another tumbler, pushing it across the cabinet towards her as if to come too close was something he wanted to avoid.

'I can't see why you're so livid with me. I assume it is with me?' she got in first before he could accuse her of anything or get to work on her with his velvety voice again. He seemed to have forgotten he had such a voice right now, for despite the whisky he threw back and the fact that his face didn't lose its wildness she waited in vain for him to say something.

Instead he went to stand at the window with a fresh drink in his hand. His broad shoulders flexed beneath the thin summer-weight linen of his jacket. The way his dark hair skimmed the top of his collar made her want to reach out and touch it, and she felt the familiar weakness in the pit of her stomach again. She had to close her eyes to stem the flood of love that swept overpoweringly through her.

'How the hell has all this got so out of hand?' His voice was savage and he didn't turn round. It was almost as if he were talking to himself. 'I've tried to work out what word it was, what gesture, what little forgotten action it was that turned your apparent love for me to this sheer, unreasoning hatred.' He turned. 'You'd have to hate me to put me through this. Was it something I did? What was it?'

She gaped at him, a look of derision bit by bit taking the place of her initial astonishment. 'Marlow...' she foundered '...if you have to ask that, what can I say?' she spread her hands. 'You can't be *serious*?'

His eyes were like marble. 'Was it the way I made love to you? Were you faking *every* time?'

She shuddered. 'You know it wasn't that,' she admitted in a small voice. Her face crimsoned, violent images of his body on and in hers shaking her control. She pushed the images to one side. 'I know what you're doing,' she said. 'If I listen to you you'll do it again. As you did before. As you always do.'

'What's that?' he demanded harshly.

'You know. It's your big talent—the way you can charm people into doing or believing anything. It's because you've been around, I suppose. But it's wicked, Marlow. If it didn't matter so much that you can make me do what I don't want to do, then it would be amusing. But it's almost evil, this ability you have to make me believe the opposite of what I know is true.'

'I don't seem to be having much success with it at the moment.' His lips were in a bitter line.

Flame finished her drink without noticing. She put the glass down carefully on the table, not intending for it to be refilled, but Marlow seemed to welcome a pause in what they were saying and quickly refilled it, seeing to his own at the same time.

'My God,' he said harshly when he picked up his glass again, 'I've drunk enough today to float a battleship! I vow I'll never go through another day like this. Just tell me what I have to do, Flame. What do I have to do?'

'We're going to be beating around like this forever, not really understanding each other,' she told him in a choky voice. 'I'm going back to England as soon as I can.'

'Running out on me again? That'll be the second time. By God, it'll be the last!' His eyes seemed to shoot blue flame at the thought. In one stride he was beside her. 'You're not going, do you understand? I shan't let you. I can stop you!'

'What?' Flame was frightened for a moment as he dragged her roughly from the chair where she was sitting, one hand coming down to finger woundingly against her throat.

'I'll keep you here, one way or another. I'll keep you here, I won't let you go——' He let his hand slide down the velvety whiteness of her neck to the curve of her shoulder and spoke rapidly as if half to himself. 'I wanted you to want me. It's true I've done everything I can to seduce you. I wanted you, I had to have you. That's why I married you—to make you mine.' Something seemed to enter his head and his expression changed.

He began to pull her body slowly, remorselessly, against his own. She could feel the evidence of his desire against her thighs, but was powerless to draw back.

He said hoarsely, 'I wanted you to want what I wanted. And there's one sure way to make you want that...' He showed her what he meant by running his hands thrillingly over her body, observing her involuntary undulation with satisfaction.

'Despite what you said about faking last night,' he went on, 'despite that, Flame, I don't think you were being completely honest, were you? I think you want me when I touch you. You always want me when I touch you. That's the only thing in all this craziness I'm sure of. I think you can't help yourself. Last night you wanted me. You weren't faking.' He paused. When he started to speak again his voice was rough with unashamed desire. 'Maybe last night you started off thinking of this other guy. But you were pretty soon thinking only of me. I'd bet a lot on it. And another thing...' By this time his hands had begun to play sweet music with her senses, touching in a way that seemed like nothing to look at but in the unseen world of feeling was playing the subtlest melody of delight. It was music she longed to hear, a respite from the pain shadowing her since last night, for she was here, he was here—and for a brief moment out of time she could shut her eyes to everything else.

But he seemed to have lost the thread of what he was saying, and only with an effort brought his mind back to it. 'Another thing,' he whispered in her hair, 'I don't think a nice guy is what you really want. I think you'd much prefer a heel like me. I'm the villain, remember? I think I'm the one you want. And if you're not convinced yet, my lovely, I'm going to convince you right now.'

'Marlow, I'm not in the mood for silly games...'

'Nor am I, baby,' he whispered in her ear. 'Games are definitely out. This is for real...'

Mesmerised by his liquid tones, by the hot breath fanning her cheek, by the lips hovering just above her own, Flame felt like a trapped creature held by the hypnotic eye of a cobra. She wanted to cry out, Don't hurt me, Marlow, not again, but her mouth opened and closed without a sound coming from it.

'I'm going to show you what love is, Flame. And when you go back to England, tomorrow, next week, whenever you decide to go back, you'll take the memory with you like a brand, a memory of love, of what it can be—and believe me, it's not going to be something you'll ever want to describe as ''nice''!'

She shuddered at the word 'love', having yearned so long to hear it on his lips, but now, when she did so, it seemed to mean something entirely different from what she wanted, and she could only stare in confusion.

He gave a sudden wrench with both hands either side of her blouse, ripping it open so that the buttons were scattered in all directions. Then his hands began to explore her naked breasts, closing familiarly over them with just the exact touch he knew she found so hard to resist. It was as if her body knew its master, opening to him, blossoming and blushing, hardening and rippling and suddenly seeking and offering the same mindless abandon, the same speech without words and the love for love that only their bodies knew how to express.

With a dull snap she heard the sound of his belt buckle, the rasp of a zip, then, without wanting it, without planning it, she felt her fingers reach out, searching to touch his warm flesh, her fingers slithering over the hard muscles of his abdomen, encountering the rough hair of his loins. His arousal was complete and vaguely frightening, as if her touch had somehow unleashed some primeval force that now had them both under its control. All attempt to resist him collapsed in an instant. She felt him hook his fingers in the waistband of her skirt and pull it off, throwing it to one side as he fully discarded his own clothes too, taking her savagely into his arms in the same movement, so that they met, skin against skin, in ecstatic contact.

She began to move uncontrollably against him as the stinging nip of his teeth over her sensitised flesh brought fresh surges of pleasure breaking over her in ever-increasing waves. He fevered kisses over her naked breasts again as if driven by a mindless frenzy of need. Their bodies seemed to melt into each other, yet it was as if such closeness was unequal to the strength of their drive to be united.

Flame closed her eyes as she felt him squeeze her waist between both his hands, smoothing and caressing it with long, slow sweeps of his palms, then bringing her whole body sliding down beneath his own. She found herself sinking back on to a wool rug on the floor. Marlow's own desire had built to match hers as he knelt over her, one knee parting her legs, making her yield with a moan of pleasure before crying out for his ultimate possession. Then he brushed her lips again and again, drinking in all their warm offering as if it were the nectar of paradise.

He took her swiftly and strongly before she could resist, the sudden union dizzying at once to the zenith of desire, sending their unisoned cries spiralling upwards. Flame fell back to earth like a wounded bird, brought down by his huntsman's aim.

She was breathless, speechless for long moments afterwards. Somehow she wanted to prolong this sweet aftermath, sucking it of every atom of bitter joy before reality closed in again, taking away as it would her reason for happiness. But Marlow hadn't finished. With a sigh of complete surrender, he guided her hands to where they gave him renewed pleasure, turning her, twisting her, flowing over her in a choreography of delicious steps that brought more pleasure than she thought she could bear.

This time their flight seemed endless, stretching the horizons of pleasure to unimagined limits. Marlow's eyes were luminous, soft as blue velvet afterwards but with lights of savage splendour in them, his strong face gentled by love, his former tension, his rage, his hardness, all washed away, leaving him open and vulnerable, like a god resting in the arms of his goddess.

Flame was confused by the change in him. As they lay together on the rug she stroked his thick, dark hair.

His eyes were closed now, stubby lashes lying defence-lessly on his cheek. She couldn't resist kissing them, making them flutter. His eyes opened.

He propped himself on one elbow. 'Now,' he said, in a flat voice, 'when you leave you'll remember.'

She wriggled from beneath him, wrenched by inner pain as her flesh tore itself free from contact with his. It was only like this—with him—that she knew she was truly alive. Only like this—with him—she found a reason for living.

'*Am* I going back?' she muttered.

'It's what you want.' He looked away.

'In that case I'd better go back to the house.'

'Wait.' He got up, unaware how her eyes dwelt for the last time on the smooth contours of his body, as he began to drag on his jeans, pulling a T-shirt over his broad shoulders and down the V-shape of his torso as casually as if to conceal himself from her was of no consequence. Flame had to stifle a cry of deprivation. Then he bent to dress her with fingers she could have believed expressed love if she hadn't known better, as he gently fastened her buttons and softly smoothed the long tresses of amber hair.

He walked to the door with her, only touching her when they reached it and then merely lifting her fingers to his lips. 'Goodbye,' he said.

She looked into his eyes, searching for some other word he could say to her, a word that would wipe out the pain forever. '*Goodbye?*' she questioned. Her heart poised on the edge of breaking into a million fragments again.

He smiled, spoke softly, kissed her fingertips. 'Farewell, my lovely,' he said with a cynical twist of his lips.

With a constriction in her throat she allowed him to turn her towards the door, then, half blind with grief, she allowed him to send her outside. The door closed almost at once. In a storm of remorse she stumbled down the path between the trees. It wouldn't be the end. He couldn't mean it. She knew she would never have been able to give herself like that if their love wasn't real. It was madness to go on hoping to be able to live without him. She belonged to him—she belonged completely and forever.

It was suppertime already, but the meal was half over before Flame dared mention Marlow's absence.

Samantha looked mystified. 'Do you know where he is, Emilio darling?'

Her husband shook his head. 'Perhaps he doesn't know the time. You know what he's like when he's stuck into some work. Want me to go over and find out, *cara*?'

'Please, dearest.' She touched his hand. He kissed her on the forehead and left.

He was back within a few minutes. 'No sign of him— he must have gone out. But his car is still here, I see.'

'Are you sure he isn't there?'

Emilio shrugged. 'The doors were open. I had a good look round—no sign. But don't worry, I expect he's gone for a walk on the beach. It's a nice way to unwind.' He looked at his wife.

Later Flame doused the candles. Marlow hadn't come up to eat with them, and when she walked over to the *casita* it was as Emilio had told them. The doors were open, but of Marlow there was no sign. Apprehensive, she returned to the villa to wait.

Midnight came.

'Best get some sleep,' advised Samantha. 'He's probably walked into town. It can be done in under an hour. He's done it before when he thinks he's not getting enough exercise.' She smiled. 'You're worried, aren't you? I thought you said you didn't care.'

'I've discovered caring is something I do a lot of where Marlow's concerned,' muttered Flame. 'I can't fight what I feel any longer. It's just no good without him.'

Samantha took her briefly in her arms. 'I know, you silly idiot. You've always loved him—we all know that. Only I wish you'd made it plainer to him. He's gone through hell.'

'I never wanted to make him unhappy. It's just what he did to me——'

'What did he do, Flame?'

Flame turned away, then she gave a little shrug. 'I suppose I may as well tell you. And maybe you'll think I'm crazy to let it mean so much. But do you remember that time I went to Ibiza to surprise him shortly after we came back from our honeymoon?'

Samantha nodded. 'It was just before you left for England.'

'Well,' Flame paused, finding the memory painful even now, 'it was me who was surprised,' she said. 'And not pleasantly... I found Victoria in his bed at the hotel. Of course, I didn't know who she was at that time.'

'In bed with Marlow?' Samantha looked shocked.

'Not exactly in with him. He'd gone out or something. But she was in his bed, very definitely.'

'I can't believe this. It was only a few days after your honeymoon...' Samantha was frowning. 'I know they've worked together for a long time, but I wouldn't have thought she was his type. I mean, they're such friends. They don't have that aura of people having an illicit affair. Are you sure about this?'

'She was in his bed, that's for sure. I recognised her the other night when she turned up with him. Then she admitted she'd worked in Ibiza. You don't imagine I'd make a mistake about it, do you?' Flame asked stiffly.

'Not about whether you saw her, no.'

'What, then?'

Samantha frowned. 'Maybe it's best if you ask Marlow point-blank what was going on. He won't lie to you.'

'Won't he?'

'Don't be ridiculous, Flame! Of course he won't. If he had anything to hide he'd damn well tell you and ask you to forgive him. You know Marlow. He'd rely on his famous charm to get him off the hook—that's if he would ever get himself into a situation like that in the first place! Oh, really, Flame, I can't believe this! Go and talk to him as soon as he comes back. Set your mind at rest, please do!'

By now Flame realised she was going to have to forget her pride and confess how she really felt. She would have to tell Marlow why she had fled to England so abruptly, and she would tell him why she had begun to suspect he had only married her to get his hands on the Montrose land—that that idea had only entered her head when she saw he was capable of adultery. She would explain how she couldn't understand how he could deceive her with another woman. It could only mean he didn't love her. And if he didn't love her there had to be a reason for marrying her. Cabo Santa Margarita was the obvious reason.

Only the problem presented by what she had been hearing in the last few days had aroused her doubts. Was Samantha wrong? And her mother? And Emilio? And all the other friends with whom Marlow seemed so popular? They didn't treat him like a land shark. It made the doubts niggle at her.

But why on earth had he married her if it wasn't for the land? She was in a quandary and couldn't see her way out.

Midnight came and went and Marlow still hadn't put in an appearance. Flame went to bed, intending to stay awake until he came back, but her eyes began to close even as she was telling herself she was only going to rest them for a minute.

Later it was the sound of rain that woke her. Not just ordinary rain, but the unleashing of tons of water from the heavens.

She lay and imagined Marlow walking through the rain as the gutters filled and all the sluices of the house rattled and gurgled with the overflow. She imagined Marlow in it, walking, walking, his dark hair shiny and wet, his white shirt sticking to his back. She wanted to go out and search for him. She wanted to bring him back home. But she didn't know where to start. And the misery of not having told him how much she loved him filled her heart.

CHAPTER TEN

WHEN Flame couldn't stay in bed any longer she went over to the *casita*, but it was obvious that Marlow hadn't been back the previous night. After last night's rain everything in the garden was steaming and a rich earthy smell filled the air. She stood under the pines and wondered what to do next. That he had said 'goodbye' filled her with a terrible dread. But before giving way to panic she had to check every avenue first. The obvious next step was to go down to the town as soon as everything opened.

Borrowing Samantha's little yellow sports car an hour or so later, she drove down the side of the hill towards the main road. There was one place he might be and one person there who might know something.

She parked outside the familiar white edifice in the town centre and took the lift to Marlow's private sanctum on the fifth floor.

The first person she met after she had talked her way through Reception was Victoria herself.

In view of the strained atmosphere at their previous meeting she was surprisingly friendly. 'Flame, how nice to see you!' she exclaimed, pausing with a bundle of files under her arm as she came out of a door on the other side of the foyer. She came straight over to her. 'Do you want to speak to Marlow? I'm afraid he's in a meeting, but I can drag him out if it's urgent.'

'A *meeting*?' Flame floundered for a moment. All the horrible, half-formed images of Marlow's body lying admid the wreckage of a car—though how, when his car was still parked outside the villa—and the hundred and one other nightmares with which she had taunted herself last night, faded, leaving only the nightmare of reality. The other woman.

'He may not be long.' Victoria flicked a glance at the clock. 'I can buzz him now if you like?'

'No, don't do that——'

'Come and have a cup of coffee with me in my office, then—you may as well wait in comfort.' Victoria had a pleasant smile. She was smiling a few seconds later as she settled Flame in a comfortable chair near her desk. 'I still feel we've met before,' she told her chattily as she dumped her files down. 'It's odd, because I've usually got an excellent memory for faces. But somehow I just can't place you.'

'I can help you there.' Flame realised she was on the brink of hearing the truth at last. Fear at having her nightmare brought into the open made her long to draw back. But it was too late for that now. 'We met in Ibiza,' she told the older woman. Her face must have looked strained, for Victoria gave a frown.

'Really? In the office, you mean?'

'No.' Flame gulped. 'Actually, you were in bed at the Hotel Excelsior.'

'Good lord, was I?' Victoria's brow furrowed.

'It was eighteen months ago.'

Victoria's mouth twitched, then to Flame's astonishment she began to laugh. 'So that's it!' she exploded. 'No wonder I'd forgotten! How embarrassing for us both! You looked absolutely stunned. I suppose you expected to find Marlow!' She bit her lip. 'I really bawled you out, didn't I? Then before I could apologise you'd gone! I was in a high old rage, I can tell you. I thought at first you were one of the staff, and the fact that you just breezed straight in really made me blow my top. I thought, this is the final straw. I've had enough!'

'I'm sorry——' Flame felt bewildered.

'Didn't Marlow tell you what happened? I expect he had far more important things on his mind just then.' Victoria chuckled again. 'I thought he was going to give me the sack! I felt awful, knowing he'd been dragged away from his honeymoon and expected everything to be set up and running like clockwork so he could get back to you. But absolutely everything went wrong that trip.'

'I still don't understand.'

'I'd been working on the new development at San Antonio, but then I was promoted to the Ibiza office. It was August. Well, you know what the island's like then. There wasn't a room to be had anywhere. I'd been hotel-hopping for two weeks and was just about at the end of my tether. Anyway, I thought I'd got Marlow fixed up—they used to keep a room free for him at the Excelsior—but just the night before he was due to turn up I had to move out of the place I was in and I simply couldn't find anywhere else. It was crazy! I decided it wouldn't matter if I stayed one night at the Excelsior, expecting to have found somewhere by the time Marlow arrived. But when he found out what had happened he told me to stay put and he'd find somewhere else. Well, of course it was impossible, but rather than give up and sleep on the beach he had his bags sent up to the room and went out again. It was about midnight by this time.

Anyway, to cut a long story short, he rang me in the
early hours to say he'd managed to find a small room
on the other side of the city and did I mind if his bags
stayed where they were till next morning. Considering
it was his room I thought he was being damned decent!
Next thing I knew you turned up.' She chuckled. 'I hope
you managed to contact him later that morning. He was
leaving for the development on the north coast and I
didn't manage to see him for another three months as
he flew back to the mainland a few days later.'

By that time, Flame remembered, she had already left
for England. She felt stunned, scarcely able to take in
what Victoria had told her.

A phone call came through and Flame took the
opportunity to think things through. Everything about
the way Victoria told her story rang true. And now,
looking at her as she spoke on the phone, Flame wondered why she hadn't thought to approach her long ago.
It was just that Victoria's fury as she had sat up in the
double bed that morning had seemed such evidence of
guilt that Flame hadn't even begun to question it.
Marlow's name was on the room and his bags were in
it. That seemed proof enough.

Now Victoria's large brown eyes were opening wide
at something she heard on the other end of the line, and
when she replaced the receiver they were brighter than
before. 'Thank heavens for that!' she exclaimed. 'Forgive
me.' She shot a quick glance at Flame. 'It's just——'
She leaned back in her leather chair and closed her eyes
for a moment, and when she opened them she gave a
huge sigh of relief. 'That was about my fiancé,' she confessed. 'He was beaten up the night before last by a gang

of youths trying to break into his car. He's been in intensive care, but he's off the danger list now.'

She pressed a buzzer on her desk. 'I think I could do with that coffee. How do you like yours?' When her secretary answered she also asked her to tell Marlow his wife was here. Then she turned to Flame.

'Marlow was a real friend the other night,' she went on. 'You remember I came dashing over at some god-awful hour to your place? It was because the hospital had told me they couldn't let me in because I'm not a relative. Marlow came back with me and soon sorted them out.' She heaved another sigh of relief. 'I've been so hellishly worried about him. He's so mad and brave, taking on four men single-handed.'

She got up as her secretary came in carrying two small cups of very black Spanish coffee. 'There now. You just sit and wait for Marlow here.' Victoria handed one cup to Flame, oblivious to the chaos of thoughts that had rendered her speechless since the bombshell of what had really happened on Ibiza hit her. But before she could bring herself to say anything the door swung in and Marlow himself stood there, looking pale, almost hollow-cheeked, his black hair accentuating his pallor. His eyes sought Flame's at once.

'Well?' he demanded. 'Come to tell me when you're leaving?'

'I—no, not at all. That isn't what I—oh, Marlow!' Somehow her coffee-cup deposited itself on the table beside her and she found herself across the room and in his arms. He drew her back into the corridor, closing the door on the two women on the other side.

'What are you trying to say?' he demanded, his eyes still lifeless as they searched her face for clues.

'I've been wrong. I don't expect you to forgive me, but Marlow, if you'll have me back, as your wife, forever—oh, please, say something, Marlow! I love you so much.' Her eyes filled and she reached up to touch his lips with the tip of one finger, wondering why she should be so incoherent when the truth was so simple to say. 'I love you, Marlow. I always have. I always have, my darling.'

He crumpled her fingers in his and held them to his lips, not saying anything, just touching them gently with the merest brush of his lips, then as time swelled and her words sank in he touched each one separately with the tip of his tongue, then kissed them properly, turning her hands over and kissing both palms, then her wrist and finally, slowly, powerfully, bringing his lips down over her mouth in a kiss that was deep and true and marked his repossession of her.

Eventually he lifted his head, and this time his eyes were bluer than the sky, bright, as if the sun were in it. His mouth quirked humorously. 'We'd better let these two out of their office, we've got them cornered!'

He opened the door and called inside, and the secretary came out, giggling and casting envious glances at Flame where she stood, still entwined in Marlow's arms, oblivious to his dignity as the boss, only the running of his hands in secret underneath her short jacket showing her that dignity was the last thing on his mind.

'I talked to Victoria,' she told him when they were safely in the privacy of his own office with orders not to be disturbed.

'What was all this about Victoria?'

'I made a horrible mistake,' she confessed. Then she told him all about it, finishing up with a shamefaced plea, 'I would hate her to know what I've been thinking about her all this time. I've been so unjust!'

'She'd think you were crazy. She knows she would never stand a chance with me.' Marlow pulled her into his arms. 'I still can't quite grasp this. This morning I was fully prepared to go over and have a word with Marcos about rushing a divorce through. I thought it was the one thing I could give you that you really wanted. I was willing to give you even that if it would make you happy.'

'Marlow, I can't bear to feel I've caused so much anguish for us both. I'm going to make it up to you, if you'll let me. It was just loving you—I think I was loving you too much. And it made me so frightened, so vulnerable. The slightest thing hurt me. And I felt so young and inexperienced. I couldn't imagine you would ever find enough in me to keep you interested. I wanted to grow up quickly just for you. Even in London I thought, everything I do is for Marlow. My course in public relations—I chose that because I thought you would approve. And my job. I wanted to be the best so that if ever—if we ever met again, you would approve of me and—well, just maybe have a little regret or two that you'd ever let me go.' Flame pressed her face against the side of his chest, feeling his heart thudding in unison with her own.

'That was the hardest part—letting you go, forcing myself to sit it out until I thought you'd had enough time to find yourself. I began to feel guilty at marrying you before you'd had a chance to do any living—do you understand?'

'I think I do. Now.' Green eyes misted as he brought his lips down to hers.

'And this guy in London——' he began tentatively, when he eventually released her.

'He never was and never could be my lover. He flirts with me and makes me laugh. He's not the man of my dreams, and never could be. He's always known it.'

'And what about this other problem? The one that makes you think I only want you for your inheritance?'

Shyly she looked up at him. 'I give you whatever I have willingly and completely, Marlow. It was base of me even to raise the subject.'

'It was relevant when you thought I didn't love you.'

She nodded.

'But now you know I love you, you feel it doesn't matter. You do know I love you, don't you?'

She looked at his blue eyes shining with tenderness into her own and had no doubt that all her fears were vanquished. Pressing her body against his told him what she felt.

'Even so,' he went on, 'I'm going to insist that proper deeds are drawn up. The Montrose land will always remain the property of you and your sister and your children in perpetuity.'

'Children, Marlow?'

'Don't you want babies?' He looked uncertain until she reached up and began to whisper little words of love as she scattered his face with kisses. 'Ask Mother and Samantha how I feel about babies,' she told him happily. 'If you feel the same way I can think of nothing more perfect than talking soft furnishings and rabbits and bows!'

*　　*　　*

It was late when they returned to Santa Margarita, to their house among the pine trees at the top of the cliff. They had been for an evening drive along the coast and Marlow had pointed out the new village he was building and various other projects that were pockets of beauty amid the contours of the hills. They came on to the terrace as everyone, including Sybilla, allowed up for the first time in weeks, was sitting down to dine.

'Welcome, darlings, just in time,' she said, taking their appearance draped in each other's arms with amazing aplomb. 'I've been looking forward to this event for a long time.' Whether she meant being allowed out of bed or seeing them both back together again no one asked. It was enough that everything was as it was.

Emilio rose to his feet and proposed a toast in rapid Spanish that was flowery and over the top and exactly what everyone felt, and they raised their glasses with many joyful clinks. Flame couldn't stop her eyes meeting Marlow's in a secret exchange. Soon there would be other reasons for family celebrations, but now it was enough to know they were together again at last.

They left everyone chatting round the dining table and strolled towards the *casita*. 'It's too beautiful to go inside yet,' murmured Marlow in Flame's ear as he began to fondle her breasts under her blouse. 'I've always thought the smell of pine needles erotic. What do you think?'

'Marlow...' She hesitated for no more than a second. 'You can still read my mind,' she told him happily, sinking down beneath him in the shadow of the trees. 'Read me forever, darling, simply forever.'

'Forever,' he murmured as the night closed round them and the soft sighing of the sea matched their own sighs of love. 'Simply forever... my lovely.'

Take 4 bestselling love stories FREE

Plus get a FREE surprise gift!